THE
EAGLE
KITE

A NOVEL BY

Paula Fox

ORCHARD BOOKS • NEW YORK

Permission to use the four lines from "Crazy Jane and
Jack the Journeyman" that appear as the epigraph on
page ix is gratefully acknowledged. Reprinted with
permission of Simon & Schuster, and A. P. Watt Ltd. on
behalf of Michael Yeats, from *The Poems of W. B. Yeats: A
New Edition,* edited by Richard J. Finneran. Copyright
1933 by Macmillan Publishing Company, renewed by
Bertha Georgie Yeats.

Orchard Books, 95 Madison Avenue, New York, NY 10016

Manufactured in the United States of America
Book design by Mina Greenstein
The text of this book is set in 12 point Baskerville.
1   3   5   7   9   10   8   6   4   2

Library of Congress Cataloging-in-Publication Data
Fox, Paula.
The eagle kite : a novel / by Paula Fox.
p.   cm.
"A Richard Jackson book"—Half t.p.
Summary: Liam's father has AIDS, and his family cannot
talk about it until Liam reveals a secret that he has tried to
deny ever since he saw his father embracing another man
at the beach.
ISBN 0-531-06892-7.   ISBN 0-531-08742-5 (lib. bdg.)
[1. Homosexuality—Fiction.   2. Fathers and sons—
Fiction.   3. AIDS (Disease)—Fiction.   4. Death—
Fiction.]   I. Title.
PZ7.F838Eag   1995
[Fic]—dc20   94-26415

For my daughter,
LINDA CARROLL

For love is but a skein unwound
Between the dark and dawn.
A lonely ghost the ghost is
That to God shall come.

—WILLIAM BUTLER YEATS

CONTENTS

ONE

The Sickness

Across the street from Liam Cormac's apartment house stood an abandoned church of crumbling brick and fieldstone. The remains of a scaffolding, erected several years earlier when there had been plans to restore the church, circled its spire. Pigeons strutted on the wooden boards of the platform and perched on the metal framework. When the wind blew fiercely from the west, gathering intensity as it dove into the constricted streets of New York City, loose boards gray with pigeon droppings clattered. Once, one had been dislodged and had fallen to the sidewalk below, narrowly missing an elderly couple walking their little dog. A neighborhood organization protested about the incident to city hall but to no avail.

"Wait until someone gets killed," Aunt Mary, his father's sister, had said grimly to Liam and his mother, Katherine, last Thanksgiving. "Then they'll do something!"

On the September day that Liam began his first year of high school, a man looking like a scarecrow came to haunt the church steps. As people passed him by, most of them averted their heads. Infrequently, someone would drop a coin into a child's blue plastic beach bucket the man placed at his feet where he crouched on the bottom step. The hood of his ragged black sweatshirt hid most of his face.

One morning, as Liam watched him from a window of his third-floor apartment, the man took from beneath his sweatshirt a piece of cardboard that he appeared to try to smooth with a wasted hand. He propped it between his knees and the bucket and settled into his customary position, his head bowed.

Liam knew what was printed on the cardboard. He had read the few words as he passed the church one day. He had glimpsed the sparse hairs of a scraggly beard, bony hands, kneecaps poking up against the worn cloth of stained cotton pants. It was the only time Liam saw the man up close.

On the days he went directly home after school, he found himself irresistibly drawn to look. An impulse would seize him. He would leave his homework, or whatever else he was doing, and go to a window to stare down at the man.

His mother would call out, "Liam! Settle down, will you, please?" It was as though he couldn't see enough of that scarecrow. His mother must have seen the man, too, but they did not speak of him to each other.

The man was there every day. He stayed until darkness came. Then he would get up slowly, put the cardboard sign back under his sweatshirt, pick up the bucket, empty out what change there was, drop it in his pocket, and shuffle down the street until he disappeared from Liam's view.

On stormy days, he sat farther up the steps, where he was partly sheltered from the rain by a stone arch above the church entrance. On those days, he kept the plastic bucket on his lap and held the sign in front of it with his fingers covering some of the words. Liam felt angry at the man. Was he stupid? Who would take the trouble

[3]

to climb up the steps and drop a coin in his bucket?

The sign read: I'M HUNGRY I GOT AIDS PLEASE

In late November, on the day Aunt Mary arrived from West Virginia to spend her second Thanksgiving with Liam and his mother, the man did not appear on the church steps.

Until it grew dark, Liam searched for him throughout the neighborhood. He went to other churches. He peered into tenement hallways and into the alleys between buildings. He checked storefront entrances. The man was nowhere to be found. Liam did not see him again.

In Springton, a village on the New Jersey shore, two hours from the city by bus, Liam's father, Philip, had been living for the past year in a small cabin. Like the man who begged on the church steps, Liam's father had AIDS.

TWO

Secrets

Liam had learned of his father's sickness on a Saturday morning a year ago, a few days after his thirteenth birthday. Philip Cormac left home early to go to the Brooklyn Botanic Garden. He was a landscape architect, and he often visited botanical sites in and around the city. Liam was to meet his best friend, Luther Fahey, at the Museum of Natural History to look at prehistoric human bones.

He had been zipping up his jacket at the front door when his mother called him from the kitchen. "Wait," she said.

"I'll be late," he shouted at her from the front door.

"Come here!" Her voice rose on the last word.

He went to the kitchen and sat down at the round table.

"Your father is very sick," she said. He gazed at her silently. Her head was bent over the table as she gathered toast crumbs with one hand. The sound irritated him.

"Why don't you use a sponge?" he asked.

She looked up. Her face was wet with tears. Her hand continued to move in ever-widening circles. A pile of crumbs rose next to her coffee cup.

"Will you please quit that!" Liam cried.

"Terribly sick," she whispered.

Fear came to him. "Mom?"

"When he had his appendix out? In the fall three years ago? So we had to cancel the trip to West Virginia to see Aunt Mary and Grandpa? You remember, Liam, don't you?"

She pressed a used paper napkin against her face. She opened her hand, and the napkin drifted to the floor. "Don't you remember that?" she cried out.

His throat had closed up. He couldn't speak.

"After the operation, he needed a blood transfusion. The blood was tainted. But we didn't know that . . . for a long while. It's very bad."

His voice came back. It was muffled as though he were speaking through a blanket. "Tainted with what? How bad?"

"I can't—," she began, then stood up, circled the table, and leaned down and put her arms around Liam. Her embrace was awkward, stiff. Her elbow pressed against his neck. He sat like a stone. "Daddy will tell you about it," she said in his ear. He felt the moisture of her breath. He heard her walk out of the kitchen. A moment later, he heard the bedroom door close shut.

Liam walked to the museum. My mind is in pieces, he said to himself. This is what it was like to be crazy, when one part of you tried to get away from all the other parts. He did not understand what he had heard, only that something terrible had happened.

As soon as he saw Luther at the museum entrance, they quarreled. Liam knew it was his own fault. Luther said, "I've changed my mind. Let's not look at those dusty old bones. Let's go to Columbus Circle and watch people. Did you know that everybody sways? I'll prove it to you—"

"We're going to do what we planned," Liam

interrupted furiously. "What do you mean people sway! You're nuts!"

"What's eating you?" Luther asked in a bewildered voice. "They do sway! I noticed it for the first time this week. I do it myself. It's because the earth wobbles."

Liam turned his back on Luther and walked into the great hall of the museum. He heard Luther behind him. "No bones for me!" he said angrily. Then he was gone.

Liam went outside and paused on the steps. Luther was loping south on the broad avenue in front of the museum. Liam had no feeling about him, about the quarrel. Luther was just a boy moving fast on his way somewhere.

He saw nothing as he walked home. He felt bodies passing him; he heard traffic, its angry snarling. Suddenly he was in front of his own apartment, his key in his hand. He inserted it and turned the lock. His mother was sitting on the couch in the living room, an unopened newspaper on her lap.

"I thought you were meeting Luther," she said listlessly.

"Are you going to tell me more?" Liam demanded.

She picked up the newspaper, then let it drop

back on the couch. "I'm not as clear about it as your father is," she said, not looking at him, her voice oddly small, almost indistinct.

"Did you just find out? You sound like you just did," he said.

"It's telling you," she said, not answering his question.

He started toward his room.

"Liam? Where are you going?"

"I've got homework," he replied harshly.

He lay on his bed, staring at the ceiling. Dread came like a slow tide, starting at his feet, closing over him.

After a while, he got up and arranged the books on his shelves in alphabetical order; then he rearranged them according to subject. He went to the kitchen and grabbed some crackers and stuffed them in his mouth. He was hungry, but he couldn't think of anything he wanted to eat. His mother was in her bedroom again. He thought of telephoning Delia, whom he loved. What would he say to her?

Their phone conversations were like a kind of singing with a repeated refrain of a few words: "What are you thinking about . . . ?" "You. . . ." When they laughed at the same time, it was as though a silk cloth had softly fallen over them.

Just after a noon whistle blew from some-where, his father came home. Liam opened his door, but Philip Cormac did not see him. He was staring at Liam's mother, who stood in the bed-room entrance.

"Katherine? Did you tell him?"

"What I could," she said.

They stood motionless, their heads bowed. The living room looked unfamiliar to Liam. It had been transformed, turned into one of those scenes he had seen on television, a picture taken after a disaster—fire or earthquake—with two sorrowful people wandering through ruins, look-ing for lost things in the debris.

His father suddenly looked up and saw Liam.

"Take him for a walk, will you?" his mother said coldly. "Don't talk to him about it here." Then, her voice louder, "Not in our home."

"Katherine," his father said, so sadly.

Silently, Liam and Philip left the apartment and walked to Riverside Park, several blocks away. A few people exercised their dogs along paths glittering with broken glass. Liam's hands were cold. He shoved them in his pockets.

He was nervous. He wished he'd gone with Luther after all. Something was coming toward him. It had no shape, but it seemed to exhale iciness like his mother's voice when she said, "Not in our home." In the weeks after his father's appendectomy three years ago, he and his mother carried tray meals to him, brought him books, held his arms when he practiced walking around the apartment until his strength came back. What Liam knew at the moment was that this time it would be different.

His father began to speak softly, as he did when Liam, on the warm mothy edge of sleep, heard him say, "Good-night, sweet Liam—funny dreams, good dreams . . ."

"The sickness I have is very bad," Philip said. "We all die. I'll die sooner."

"Sooner," echoed Liam. He clenched his jaws to keep his mouth from trembling.

"No one knows, no one can predict when. It could be a year, eight years. What I've got is called acquired immune deficiency syndrome."

Fear unfurled in Liam like a great banner. He was frightened by the wind from the river, the bounding black dog he glimpsed on a playground, the heavy monotone of traffic on Riverside Drive, but most of all, by the way his father's words reached his ears as though they traveled from a great distance.

"When your immune system doesn't work, you

lose protection against all kinds of diseases, pneumonia, cancer, tuberculosis. Syndrome means—"

"AIDS," said Liam.

His father sat down abruptly on the bench next to which they had paused. "Yes," he said. "Well, I supposed you would have known about it. Everyone does now."

Liam had read a story only last week in a newspaper about a boy in a town in the South who had AIDS, how other parents in the school he went to said he should be kept at home, and how, finally, the kid's house was set on fire in the middle of the night and the kid and his family had to move away. Where did you go when your house was burned down?

His father was telling him what he'd seen at the botanic garden that morning. Liam sat at the other end of the bench. His father's hands were gripped in his lap as he spoke of the ginkgo tree. It had existed in the Triassic period and had been saved from extinction by Buddhist monks. Liam had learned the Latin names of plants long before he knew the common ones. Often his father had taken him to sites where he was working.

Once, he remembered, his father had told him, "The earth is so intimate when you touch it and lie upon it. It's a body. It seems to breathe. The whole earth breathes."

Liam wanted to cry out loud. But there were no words for what he felt.

How was it they were sitting on the bench like two acquaintances who might, or might not, talk to each other?

He hadn't asked Liam what he knew about AIDS. He hadn't said anything about tainted blood transfusions. But if he had, Liam would have known his father was lying to him just as his mother had lied to him.

Blood transfusions were safe now. They had been safe for years. Liam knew that from the sex-education class in school, what Luther called, "Learning how if you're so dumb you didn't guess."

"They burned down somebody's house because their kid had AIDS—they made them leave the place where they lived," Liam burst out.

"The stupid and cruel love their stupidity," his father said. "It gives them immense power. Let's go home now. Do you want to ask me anything?"

Philip turned and held out his hand as though he wanted Liam to take it. Liam couldn't.

"How long have you had it?" he asked.

"I'm not sure," his father said, his voice calm, as though he were continuing to talk about the history of a tree. He was staring at a nearby maple, at its few yellowed leaves. "I've had a related illness, HIV, for quite some time. Then it changed into this other thing a short while ago."

They both stood up. They walked home as silently as they had gone to the park.

Liam was thinking about the past year, about how he had noticed things without questioning what they meant—his father's increasing thinness, how often he came home early from his office to rest in the afternoons, his frequent colds and fevers.

There had been something else. It had weighed on Liam, but each day when he went to school, he had thrown off the weight, left it at home. The three of them weren't together as they had been. At supper, each of them gave reports of the day, his about school, Daddy's about some job he was doing in Westchester, Mom's about the classes she was taking to become a librarian.

When the reports were over, the dishes washed and dried and put away, each of them went off to his or her room and closed the door.

Liam had been glad. In a way, he wasn't very

interested in his mother and father—not the way he always had been. He guessed it was partly because of Delia, who had come to live in his mind and in his dreams at night.

They stood at the door to the apartment. His father said, "Please. Look at me." Liam turned to him but took a step backward. "I know how terrible this news is that I've given you," Philip said. "There was a moment in the last two weeks when I thought I wouldn't tell you at all. But I knew that would be worse—when you found out."

"You weren't on drugs or something?" Liam asked. As he waited for his father to answer him, he felt a faint stirring of hope that he would say, "*Yes* . . . yes, I'm a heroin addict."

His father stretched out his arms toward him. Liam moved farther away. "No drugs," said Philip curtly. He unlocked the door and they went in.

FOR A FEW DAYS, Liam forgot his father and the sickness for moments at a time—when he was working on a math problem or reading a story that absorbed him, hanging around with Luther, and especially when he looked at Delia in the classes he had with her.

But before he fell asleep at night, he felt a

black panic that enclosed him like hot tar. Once, just at dawn, he awoke hearing his mother cry out, "Do you know what you've done to me? To Liam?"

He opened his bedroom door. The apartment was silent. In the living room, the lights of passing cars flickered and faded on the white walls. He felt his beating heart, a thumping in his throat.

He went back to his bed and fell into a dozy half dream of himself on a hospital gurney when he was six, felt the gurney move slowly as his mother leaned over him, murmuring something, as his father rested his hand on Liam's brow and an attendant began to draw him farther away to the operating room, where his tonsils were to be removed, and the coverlet of drowsiness, induced by a drug they had given him, lay over his terror, muffling it, as he was pushed into a white room, where he fell into the eye of a huge radiant light.

He started and woke up completely. The room was pale with gray daylight. Rain tapped against his window. For a short while he was comforted, shut in by rain, warm beneath his old red blanket.

Only a few days later, there was another shock. The three of them had finished supper. There had been no conversation at all that night.

Then Philip said, "Liam, I'm going away for a bit. Not far. Do you remember Springton, where we once rented a cottage for two weeks, a couple of years ago?"

"It's almost Thanksgiving!" Liam cried out, thinking to himself, Half-wit! What's the difference!

"It's better for all of us," his mother said.

They're enemies, Liam suddenly knew.

"Better? Why?" he asked. They wouldn't tell him. They were going to lie.

"There's a good doctor down there in the Springton hospital. He's a specialist in what I've got. I need to be near a hospital. And I'll be able to work on a book I've been thinking about."

"There are hospitals here! What book?" Liam demanded. His mother rose and began to take plates and cutlery to the sink.

"A history of botanical gardens."

"You can write a history here," Liam cried.

There was a clatter of knives and forks falling into the porcelain sink.

"Liam. I need to be by myself. It takes all my strength to live with this thing I've got. After a while, you and Mom can visit. It's not a long bus ride, about two hours. I'll need the car to get to Springton from the cabin I rented—"

[17]

"What cabin?" Liam shouted his question, frantic. "When did you rent a cabin?"

His mother began to weep. For a moment, Liam felt quieted, as though her tears were falling inside him, cooling a fever.

"Could you *not* cry?" his father pleaded.

"Oh? It's the time to laugh?" his mother exclaimed.

"Who knows?" Liam asked. "Does everybody know?" He imagined the burning house in the Southern town, the boy with AIDS and his family in their nightclothes, carrying whatever they'd been able to rescue from the flames.

"Your aunt Mary," his father said. His mother held her face in her hands. "A few old friends. Not Grandpa. He can't remember anything now anyhow."

"What do I say about you?" Liam asked. It was as though the three of them were conspirators.

His mother and father spoke at the same moment.

"AIDS," Philip said.

"Cancer," Mom said.

There was a stricken silence. His father reached out and touched Liam's hand. Liam snatched it away and got up so quickly, he overturned his chair. No one spoke as he righted it. He went to his bedroom.

In the end, he lied, too. He told Luther and Delia that his father was very sick, a kind of cancer. Delia cried and leaned her head against his shoulder. He held himself stiffly. He'd extracted tears from her with a lie. He hated himself.

IT WAS TWO MONTHS before Liam and his mother visited Philip Cormac in his rented cabin a mile or so from Springton. After that they went regularly once a month to see him. Liam didn't ask why the visits started so long after his father moved away. He didn't want to watch his mother's scared eyes as she cooked up some story to tell him.

In the cabin, his mother always made large quantities of vegetable soup, most of which she stored in the small freezer of the refrigerator while his father pretended to read a book. Liam noticed he never turned a page. There wasn't much conversation.

Liam spoke carelessly about school, making up things. He was bored and frightened at the same time. He longed to be on the bus heading home. He shut his ears when his parents spoke to each other. He felt he was in a play in which the three of them said words someone else had written. It was the same when he talked to his father on the telephone from New York. When the visits were over, when he and Mom settled into the cracked plastic seats of the bus, and the driver worked the gears and headed north, Liam was nearly happy.

In the summer of that year, Philip was in the Springton hospital for a month with pneumonia. Katherine visited him once. Liam talked to him on the phone. His father's voice was scratchy like a defective tape. "I think I saw an eagle yesterday from my window," he told Liam.

Liam was silent. Three years ago, when they rented the cottage in Springton, he had taken with him a kite shaped like an eagle. When he heard *eagle*, a door in his memory cracked open. What he saw beyond the door grew clearer every moment like a photograph negative in a developing tank.

"There aren't eagles down there," he said gruffly.

"It could have been a falcon," his father's voice rasped.

"I've got to go," Liam said, and hung up the phone.

* * *

HIS FATHER HAD GIVEN him the eagle kite for
his tenth birthday. They had taken their two-
week vacation in the cottage in August. Early one
morning, Liam set out for the beach, carrying the
kite. He hadn't had a chance to fly it until then.
The city parks were full of trees in whose
branches the kite could have become entangled.

A west wind blew steadily, raking the tall dune
grass. The glint of sun on the water made daggers
of light. Liam had the flying line wound around
a bobbin he carried in one hand, the other fingers
bunched carefully on either side of the kite's
crosspiece. The thin brilliantly colored paper rustled and crackled in the wind.

It was too early for swimmers or sunbathers.
Far in the distance, Liam saw a man walking a
dog on a leash at the water's edge. The dog would
dash forward to snap at the foam left by the
waves, dragging the man with him.

He came to a place where the dune rose
abruptly, then folded back on itself, making a
kind of shadowed passage. Liam smiled when he
saw his father standing at the passage entrance,
gazing into it. He could recall the pleasure he
had felt finding him there. He had thought he'd
gone into the village for groceries, or to the

brightly painted farm stand not far from the cottage.

An instant later, his father drew to himself, as though from the wall of hard-packed sand, a long pale arm whose covering of blond hairs Liam could see from where he stood. His father draped the arm around his own shoulders like a scarf of flesh, then leaned forward and pulled into the light a young fair-haired man in bathing trunks who rested his head against his father's neck. Liam saw his father place one hand on the man's head and press him so close it seemed only one person stood there. Liam must have made some sound carried to his father by the wind.

Philip Cormac turned and saw him. The young man sprang backward into the passage, his disappearance marked by a thin shower of sand. Philip started to walk quickly in Liam's direction.

Liam ran down the beach. A gull cried somewhere. His fingers broke through the paper of the kite. He dropped it on the sand. He caught sight of a flight of wooden steps, and he raced up them, gulping for air, until he reached a narrow platform halfway to the top of the dune.

He paused, tried to catch his breath, heard

himself groan. There was no one now on the beach. He stared at the vast platter of the Atlantic Ocean with its crinkled rim of sand.

No distant blur of sail or bulk of working boat broke the line of the horizon. The world was empty.

It might have been a solar wind that blew against his face and ruffled his hair, stirred the raggedy, tangled carpet of orange daylilies that grew on either side of the steps. For a moment, he could not recall a human face. His hands, gripping a wooden railing, looked strange to him, as though they belonged to somebody else.

He turned and stared up at a huge frame house that the steps led to. "A Victorian pile" was how his father had described it only yesterday as they took a twilight walk on the beach.

His father told him everything—about the Hanging Gardens of Babylon, about desert plants that sent their roots miles to find water, about how pearls grew in oysters, about the dangerous, interesting world beyond the rooms of their apartment, their neighborhood, their country. He had read Liam a thousand books, and kissed his head and eyelids before he tucked him beneath his blanket at night.

He had drawn pictures of a tiny fetus at stages of its development, right up to the moment when it squirmed, howling, from the womb into the world.

"You were really pissed off," his father had told him, grinning. "I saw your little ancient man's face, all squinched up. Yelling. That's how we all come—pissed off to find ourselves in this cold world."

In this way, Liam had learned of his beginning. In this way, too, he had learned the sound of truth, a larger thing, a presence existing beyond all facts, all opinions—the truth in his father's voice speaking from the deepest part of himself.

But his father had not spoken of men who loved each other as men and women were supposed to. Yet, in a way he did not understand, Liam had known something about that for a long time. Other children had spoken of it. He had heard, without much interest, discussions of it on television. He had seen articles in newspapers. There was a word, *gay*. Once that word had meant merry, lighthearted. The meaning of words could dissolve, change.

He knew other words, the ones kids sometimes called one another for the angry thrill of it—*faggot* and *fairy*, *pansy* and *queer* and *dyke* and *nellie*. Fighting words.

He glanced up at the old house. It looked empty, but there might be someone inside it, waiting for him to take one more step up and become a trespasser so that someone could shoot him.

After a while, he went down to the beach and headed toward home. He caught sight of the kite where he had dropped it on the sand. The paper popped and rippled in the wind like a small fierce fire. He tore off the eagle's yellow beak and threw it into the water, and then, without knowing why, he dug a hole, smashed the crosspiece, and buried it all, colored paper and laths and string and bobbin.

His father arrived home an hour or so after he did, his arms loaded with bags of groceries. His mother was frying chicken for a picnic they planned to take to the beach later on.

Philip didn't look at him right away. But as Liam stood at a window, watching cardinals fussing at the bird feeder outside, he suddenly appeared at his side. "That was a friend I ran into . . . Geoff," he said.

Ran into, Liam thought, and felt his mouth twist. He said nothing.

That evening, as the three of them sat on the beach, a fire of driftwood warming their legs,

Liam felt he was saying good-bye to them. Something had happened. It was as though he were remembering them from a past time.

He had tried telling himself that Geoff *was* his father's friend. He had seen men hug each other before.

But, oh! Not like that! He drew away from the fire just as his mother reached for his hand. "It's so lovely here," she murmured. "Look at the moon. It's nearly full." Liam buried his hands in the cool sand. He raised his head and saw his father staring at him, his eyes sockets of darkness.

LATER, ON THE DAY that his father had left the apartment carrying two suitcases and a duffel bag, two years and three months after that picnic on the beach, Liam made the first of several visits to the public library in his neighborhood. Each time he took from the shelf the same heavy medical encyclopedia. The pages he studied were smudged, he was sure, with his own fingerprints.

He flinched when he looked at the photographic plates that showed ailing human bodies in violent colors. He read more and more about his father's illness. On the fourth afternoon, he came across the words *brain seizures*, and he fled the library, leaving the encyclopedia on a table, and went into a small Greek fast-food place a block from home, where he drank cups of black coffee until it grew dark.

He was thinking, his stomach fluttering as caffeine washed through it in thick waves, how he had managed to forget for so long what he had witnessed on the beach. He couldn't recall the name of the man his father had embraced, although on the evening of the picnic, he had thought he would never forget it.

By the time school started that year, he had slid back, so easily it now seemed, into his familiar life. The summer vacation in the cottage in Springton had dropped away just as a book in which he had found nothing to interest him might have fallen from his hand.

Yet all the time, the memory of what he had seen on the beach had remained, coiled, in his head. Now it had unwound, sprung up like a jack-in-the-box, every detail of it as clear as it had been when the sea wind had rustled the paper of the eagle kite as he stood frozen, looking at his father and a man locked together as though nothing could separate them.

He had broken and buried the kite. Nothing

much of it would have survived the years. He had buried the memory. Everything of it had survived.

He thought of the sex-education classes in school, in which what he heard had a peculiar familiarity like faces in dreams that you know but can't name. After the classes Luther would make him laugh, and their hilarity would release them from the room of facts and embarrassment.

"Now, children!" Luther would say solemnly. "Don't ever be naughty. There's death in these here parts!"

They would walk away from school, bent over with laughter. "They're doing *it*," Luther would say, pointing up at the window of some building.

"That's an office!" Liam would cry.

"Everywhere—they're always doing it," Luther would intone. "Between wars, what else is there to do?"

With Delia, it was different. If they spoke to each other in the corridor right after the sex class, there was a strangeness between them, a sense that they were nothing more than the bodily parts the teacher had drawn on the blackboard, that could make babies or kill with disease.

Why did the teacher smile as she wrote the words *needles*, *blood*, *bodily fluids* in differently colored chalk? She spoke so cozily. Teddy bears having sexual intercourse. Sex wasn't cozy. It was a precipice that drew you to its edge, closer, closer.

The next day, the fifth and last that he went to the library, he found *brain seizures* again. He couldn't read what was written there.

The knowledge he had gained stuffed his mind. Luther's jokes didn't penetrate it any more than did confidences exchanged with Delia. He could never tell them what he knew about his father.

There was no one who would answer the questions that haunted him.

Had his father done it once with the man on the beach? Had there been other men? Why had he gotten married? Was it that he had wanted to try *that*, too? He had, after all, done it with *her* once. "Because I'm here," Liam said aloud. A man reading a newspaper on the opposite side of the library table looked at him disapprovingly.

"So I see," he said.

Liam returned the encyclopedia to its place on the shelf and went home.

"Hello, darling," his mother called out from the kitchen. He went straight to his room. His father would die.

A thought came to him, so terrible a thought, he flew to the kitchen. His mother was scrubbing small red potatoes with a brush at the sink.

"Are you all right?" he cried.

Startled, she dropped the potatoes and turned to him.

"I mean—you're not sick, too, are you?"

She studied his face for a moment. Then she went to him and took his shoulders in her hands. "I am absolutely all right," she said forcefully.

THE SECOND THANKSGIVING of his father's absence had come. Aunt Mary arrived two days before the holiday, complaining about the fresh chestnuts and pecan pie she had had to carry along with her luggage. She announced that the nurse she had found to stay with Liam's grandfather while she was away wore too much makeup. She taught chemistry at a junior college in West Virginia. Liam could imagine her classes—formulas hurled like thunderbolts at students crouching at their desks.

"You need family around you in these troubled times," she had insisted last year.

In the old days before his father's illness, when his mother still spoke to Liam about her thoughts and feelings, she had once said she didn't like

Aunt Mary one bit, but you had to put up with people in your family, even when a relative was a crocodile.

Liam had discovered some time ago that if he said, "You're right," to whatever his aunt said, she'd leave him pretty much alone.

"My sister belongs to the blamist party," his father had once told him. "She found out when she was about five—when I was born, as a matter of fact—that you can blame other people for everything rotten that happens to you. It's a quick fix for making your life simple."

One day before Thanksgiving, Liam woke and sat straight up in his bed. He wanted desperately to see Daddy.

During the year he'd been away, Liam had had no desire to see him at all, not even to talk to him on the telephone. The visits he'd made with his mother to the cabin in Springton had been wearying and lifeless. They were always followed by a kind of self-disgust in Liam, as though he'd cheated on a test or lied stupidly about something that hardly mattered.

Now he heard Aunt Mary rearranging the furniture in the living room. She was a person who always had a better idea than anyone else had.

Barefoot, in his pajamas, he went to the kitchen.

"Wear slippers," Aunt Mary called after him.

"I want to see Daddy," he said to his mother.

"Well—you can see him. We'll go down in a week or so," his mother said in a vague voice. She was staring at a small turkey in a plastic bag that lay on the counter. "It'll never thaw," she muttered.

"I mean today," Liam said.

"I don't know about the bus schedule," his mother said.

"There are buses all the time. Can I?"

She turned and clasped her hands and stared down at the floor. "All right," she said. "Do what you want."

"Maybe he really was a dope addict. Maybe he got it from a needle, and you don't want to tell me that!" he cried.

"From the blood transfusion," she said as though reciting a rule she might forget at any moment.

She raised her head. Her blue eyes, so like his own, gazed at him with apparent calm. "I'm sorry," he muttered for no reason he could think of. She reached out and touched his cheek with her fingers. He realized how rarely she touched him anymore.

"I'm glad you're going to see him—if that's what you want to do," she said. She glanced away for a moment. She whispered in the direction of a narrow broom closet, "He must be lonely."

At that moment, Aunt Mary plodded into the kitchen.

"I want you to get some brussels sprouts, Liam," she commanded. "How did the sprouts get forgotten?" she asked the room. "Well, Liam?"

"Liam's going to Springton to see his dad," his mother said.

"I'm absolutely against it!" Aunt Mary cried. "I've always been against it. And I've dragged all this food up from home for tomorrow! You're not going to stay overnight down there, are you? What about the trouble I've gone to for our Thanksgiving?"

"I don't know if I'll stay the night," Liam said.

"No one has proved you can't get that revolting disease from drinking glasses and utensils. You should make your own meals while you're there. Take a towel from here! Really, Liam! You might think of our feelings!"

"Mary!" His mother's voice sounded like a trumpet call. "Why is it that you dig up the stupidest things people tell you? What are you saying? How dare you presume I'd let Liam be exposed if there was any danger?"

Liam had to press one bare foot on the other to stop himself from jumping around in a crazy way. He was suddenly happy! He'd forgotten what it was like—to be with his mother in this way, united, defended.

Aunt Mary looked bewildered, if only for a moment. She said sullenly, "You can probably get it from tears."

"Tears!" exclaimed his mother. She shook her head as though in disbelief at her sister-in-law's words. But then her shoulders slumped, and she turned to the counter to press a finger against the turkey's breast.

"Tears, tears!" Aunt Mary repeated impatiently. "When people cry."

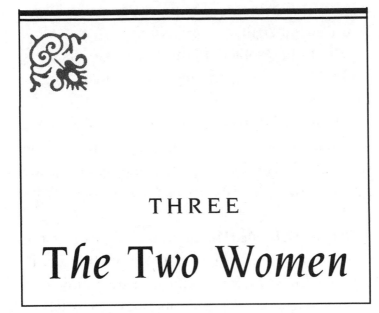

THREE
The Two Women

"Well—and how are the two women?"

"Okay."

"You're some great reporter."

"I'm not a reporter," Liam said. He dropped his backpack on the bare floor of the cabin. Dust rose and settled.

"Everyone is a reporter in one way or another," his father said. "Your face tells me they're grim."

"If I look grim, it's because of the way you ask about them. Why do you call them 'the two women'? It's Mom and your sister, Aunt Mary. You remember them, don't you?"

His father smiled faintly. A large black cat waddled into the room and sat down, staring at Liam.

"Where did you get *that*?" he asked. But why had he spoken so scornfully? Why had he come at all? He felt his glance sliding about the room as though his eyes had come loose from his head.

"That is Julius. He came tearing out of the woods a month or so ago, just after your last visit. He was thin as a wire, and a large yellow dog was chasing him, snapping its fangs." His father paused and drew a deep breath. "I named him after you."

As far back as Liam could recall, his father had made such jokes, crazy jokes that used to make him laugh wildly just because there was no explanation for them. He didn't laugh now. The joke—if that's what his father thought it was— was senseless.

"You feed him too much," Liam said. "He's the fattest thing I ever saw."

"Somebody has to eat around here," his father said mildly. "I ordered take-out for our supper right after you phoned."

Liam shrugged. He didn't care about food. He didn't want to talk about food.

"But really—how are they? Is your mom holding up against Aunt Mary destroying the furniture?"

"What do you care?" Liam burst out. "They won't ask me about you!"

"I bet they won't!" his father said sourly.

They had never talked to each other this way. The visits with Mom had been polite and soft and dim. But now he felt the way he had one late bitterly cold afternoon when he'd taken a shortcut home from school across an empty lot and seen a figure covered with rags rise up like an apparition from the weed- and garbage-covered broken earth and wave its arms at him. The very air of the cabin felt raw and chill. If he left now, he knew he'd not be able to come back again.

He looked at his father directly for the first time.

Philip was sitting in a brown wicker chair that creaked with his every slow movement. His hair, once so thick, was like a handful of dry straw. His nose looked longer, his teeth larger. But it was his thinness, the flesh barely covering his bones, that made Liam's heart grip in his chest.

He had told Liam on the phone that he

wouldn't be able to meet him. So Liam had walked the mile or so to the cabin, looking at nothing, kicking the road, wondering at the impulse that had brought him to Springton.

"Am I supposed to walk into town and get the take-out?" he asked. He tried to keep his voice low, ordinary.

"I'll be better by the time we should go," his father said. "I wasn't feeling so good this morning."

The cabin was barely furnished. Between two small windows stood a cot covered with a dark gray blanket. There were a few wooden chairs, a table, a small sofa bed draped with a faded green cotton spread, and two architect lamps craning from a wall like nosy people peering over a fence. The shade on a standing lamp was torn. Against one wall of the room was a sketchy kitchen. What seemed like dozens of medicine bottles were lined up on an open shelf above a small sink. A few garments drooped from nails on another wall. There was a brown tweed jacket Liam remembered. A door led to a bathroom with a toilet and shower.

There was beauty in the landscape Liam could glimpse through the windows, a farm field, islands of trees, leafless now, and the heavy branches of a tall blue spruce that stood outside the cabin door. A few hundred feet from the cabin, the tea-colored waters of an inlet wound to the ocean a half mile away.

There were piles of books on chairs, on the floor. Liam bent to pick one up. It was a collection of poetry by William Butler Yeats.

Philip was staring at Liam's backpack. Liam grabbed it and took it to the sofa bed, where he dropped it. As he passed the round table, he ran his hand across it. Dust.

"Have you talked to Mom about Ireland? I've been working out the trip ever since we spoke about it last month. I've figured out what we can do in a week. The sooner I make airplane reservations, the cheaper they'll be. Your spring break isn't that far away."

Liam had forgotten all about Ireland, all about the conversation they had had on the telephone. He hadn't even mentioned it to his mother.

"How can you go anywhere?" Liam asked.

"I'm better than I was last week. It's the nature of this thing—you can be so awfully sick, then you get better."

"You look worse than when Mom and I came last time."

"What a brute you can be, Liam!"

Liam's throat seemed to hollow out and go dry. He stood without speaking, his bones like lead.

After a moment, his father said, "I'm sorry. You're not a brute. I am. Sickness changes a person."

"Okay," Liam said, his voice just above a whisper. He turned his back to his father.

"Liam, please . . . I'm really sorry I spoke that way. I only want you to understand that I will get better. I've thought so much about this trip, you and me. We'll go to Clare and Galway. I want to see the tower where Yeats lived. In Ireland, they call it 'tour.' It's right beside a river. And we'll go to his grave and to pubs in Sligo, and a few days in Dublin so we can walk around St. Stephen's Green. . . ." His voice was thinning, running out. It stopped all at once.

Liam sat down next to his backpack on the sofa bed.

After a while, his voice stronger, his father said, "I want us to do something together." He plucked at the cloth of his chino trousers. "If it's possible." Then, with sudden irritability, he said, "I don't want your mother along this time."

Liam watched how slowly he stood up. "I really am better. I'm trying a new drug." He walked to the kitchen counter and pointed at a pot. "I actually made soup yesterday. And I have a loaf of very good bread if you're hungry after your walk. I should have asked you sooner. . . . There's a very good baker and cook in Springton. That's where we'll get supper. And there's a place near here I want you to see. I found it when I was walking one day. My God, it's Thanksgiving tomorrow, isn't it? I keep losing track. It was so good of you to come to see me—though maybe you won't mind missing Aunt Mary shouting at the turkey to cook itself properly."

Liam didn't know whether he'd stay the night. Julius suddenly sped across the cabin floor and leaped to the sofa.

His father let out a small gasp of laughter. "Poor Julius. He clears off when I start moving. I've stepped on him a few times."

He opened the tiny refrigerator beneath the stove and turned back into the room, holding a long loaf of bread. "See? It's like the bread you can buy in Paris," he said.

There were tears running down his cheeks. He brushed his face with one hand.

"Someone I know died a while ago," he said. "A friend." He sighed and put the loaf back inside the refrigerator. "Let's sit down. Did you want to try the bread?"

"Don't open the refrigerator again," Liam said. "I'm not hungry." He went to the table and pulled out a chair and sat down, his father sitting across from him.

"Who died?" Liam asked. "What friend?"

His father got up, took out the loaf once more, and held it out to Liam. "Please. Break off a piece. It's really good." Reluctantly, Liam tore off the heel and chewed it. His father was wiping his face with both hands now. "A young friend," he said in a muffled voice. He watched Liam closely as though waiting for a significant judgment about the bread. When he spoke, his voice was stronger. "Anything interesting in school these days?" he asked.

"Science," Liam replied.

"Isn't the bread good?"

Liam thought he might go crazy if his father said *bread* one more time. "It's okay," he said.

"Anything you'd care to add about school?"

"We get searched for weapons."

"Every day?"

"Spot checks."

"You must think the world is a war. How do the kids feel about that?"

"I don't know. They found three knives on one guy. He said he had to be ready."

"For what?"

"They never say."

They fell silent. Liam had trained himself to move across the surface of their time together like a cautious ice skater. It was different today. He sensed a widening hole in the ice. He and Daddy could fall through it into the deathly cold water.

"Listen!" his father said suddenly, holding a finger to his lips. "Can you hear it? That drone like sleepy bees?"

Liam did.

"Those are molecules. Someone named Brown discovered them, so, of course, they're called Brown's molecules. They knock against one another. You can't always hear them. It's a comfort finding out things, and finding out how much you don't know."

"Yeah," said Liam. "I know people who get a lot of comfort out of not knowing anything."

"That's not what I meant."

Liam had known that. He said nothing for what seemed an hour.

"Liam? Will you talk to me?"

"Arf! Arf!" Liam barked, and got up from the table abruptly.

A while later, as he stood staring out a window, he heard his father moving about the room, hesitantly, like a very old person. He felt a flash of pity. But his mother's words, heard in the night, came back to him. *Do you know what you've done to me? To Liam?*

He hadn't come down here to feel sorry for his father.

He turned to see him pulling on the sleeves of a thick sweater. When he saw Liam looking at him, he smiled in the old way, tenderly, with a kind of—what? Challenge?

"Did you notice the sun has come out? I'm ready to go for a drive now. I want to show you something. Are you ready?"

"Does it matter if I'm ready?" Liam asked.

His father leaned against the wall among the clothes hanging from the nails.

"I've never in my life had anyone so angry at me as you are," he said in a matter-of-fact voice. "Not counting my sister. Liam. I didn't choose to leave this life."

"Could we go now?" Liam asked. In his own ears, he sounded three years old.

DOWN WHERE THE INLET BROADENED, narrow blacktop roads wound through farms and among reeds and patches of woods. The reeds bent to the wind. Because Philip was driving so slowly, Liam could hear the rustle of their long fronds. They brushed away his fretful, nervous thoughts that had, since his arrival at the cabin, been unable to form one simple thing he could state to Philip. He had been fresh, balky, sneering. Now there was only the soft rhythmic whispering outside the car, along with the low monotone of the engine. His father's thin wrists protruded from the sweater sleeves. His long thin fingers rested lightly on the steering wheel.

Years later, whenever Liam saw reeds bending over a narrow country road, he would recall this pause, moments of quietness, when he'd been emptied out of anger and pity.

"I've taken two wrong turns," his father said. "I think I do it on purpose to stay longer near the reeds. I love them so—genus *Phragmites*. There it is." He gestured with one hand toward three small Cape Cod saltboxes that sat prissily on their lots. The road was about to end in sand. Liam could see the autumnal sea, the color of gun-metal. The sky had clouded up again; the sunlight was weak.

His father parked on a grassy verge across from the cottages. A sloping path led through a stand of trees. A historical marker stood where it began. Liam read: SLAVE GRAVEYARD: IN 1847, HERE WERE BURIED ELWOOD BECKER AND HIS WIFE, LETITIA, AND, AT THEIR REQUEST, THEIR 19 SLAVES.

"I didn't know they had slaves this far north," Liam said.

"There was slavery nearly everywhere—from the beginning of human community. I read somewhere that ten thousand Greeks were sold into Roman slavery on one afternoon on the island of Delos in Greece, thousands of years ago."

They started to walk down the path. Liam suddenly recalled a curious story Philip had read to him several years ago. It had told of an old Amazonian Indian who had captured an English explorer and forced him to read all of Charles Dickens's novels over and over again. He was about to ask his father the title of that story, and the writer's name, but found he couldn't. He rarely, except by accident, referred to the time before Philip had told him of his sickness.

They arrived at a small white picket fence

bolted on either end to two large boulders. An oblong space was enclosed by a dry-stone wall, itself enclosed by evergreens and maple and oak trees. Two small crumbling tombstones stood like sentries. Before them, at intervals, were nineteen rough stones, the kind you could have found in a field.

A heavy silence was gathered there, a hush. Liam listened as though something might speak to him. The bare branches of the deciduous trees rattled faintly. He and his father leaned against the picket fence.

After a while, Philip went back up the path. Liam lingered. He looked at each unhewn stone, at the two small tombstones. He was trying to gather up the whole place to keep in memory. It was haunted, echoing with lives now gone and all their suffering.

At the thought of remembering the graveyard later, the knowledge of his father's death that was to come struck him with such force that he fell forward against the sharp fence stakes, and the pain they caused made him rear back. He wanted to get away now, and he ran up the path to the car.

His father sat in the driver's seat, the door open, smoking a cigarette.

"Since when do you smoke?" Liam asked.

"I just took it up," Philip said coolly.

Liam got into the car. How dare his father speak to him that way? It was his fault. He'd brought this terrible thing into all their lives, that forced everyone to tell lies and be alone in fear.

Philip drove fast along the roads among the reeds. The cigarette had gone out but still hung from his lips. He parked on the dirt road behind the cabin, turned off the motor, and seemed to throw himself out of the car only to fall against it limply.

"Are you okay?" Liam questioned, alarmed, imagining an ambulance drawn up to the cabin, his father on a stretcher.

"Of course I'm all right," Philip replied irritably. "I wanted to get home. That's all."

Liam kicked at the dirt road. Dust and sand flew up into the air. "Why are you yelling at me?" he demanded.

"I wasn't yelling," said his father. "I don't want to be asked if I'm all right a hundred times."

"What are we going to do now?"

"What did you expect? There's no television. Pretty soon we'll go into Springton and pick up our supper. We might even have a conversation. At the moment, I have to lie down."

Liam kicked at the road again. His father started toward the cabin. Suddenly he turned. "Don't do that," he said.

"Why not?"

His father stared angrily at him.

"Because it bothers me," he said.

His chino pants had slipped down to his hips. His shoes looked too big for his feet. Liam could see the cords of his neck muscles.

They seemed to be facing each other across an empty world into which, slowly circling, a brown leaf from a nearby tree fell at Liam's feet. He kicked again at the road, violently. A cloud of dust rose up and then settled.

"Liam!" His father's voice rang like a shot. All at once, he clutched his waist and crouched.

He looked like a dwarf with features carved cruelly by a knife.

A hood seemed to slip over Liam's head. He heard shouting. It was his own voice.

"I know how you got it! I saw you on the beach with that man. Hugging. Hugging! You all lie. Everybody is lying, lying! You know I saw you! You know it!"

His voice, which had begun to deepen this last year, cracked, and to his horror, it rose high, a small child's screech of temper.

His father slowly straightened up and stood unmoving, his expression unreadable.

"You don't know anything," he said quietly.

Gasping, Liam said, "I know everything."

"Nothing."

"You killed our family." Tears burned his cheeks. For a moment, silence closed them in. He could hear their breathing.

His father said, "Nobody is killed except me."

Liam kicked again and again at the dirt until a wall of dust rose and held between where he and his father stood. It was as though a horse had galloped frantically between two fires.

"Your own sister won't have anything to do with you because you're an old queer. . . . What about my mother! What about her? Has she got it? Have I got it?"

"No," said his father, and walked away to the front of the cabin.

"Damn Ireland!" Liam shouted at his retreating back. "Damn Yeats and Ireland!"

Liam yanked open the car door and flung himself into the backseat. His nose was running. He raked his face with open fingers. He heard himself whimper. His fingers were wet and sticky, and he wiped them on his jacket. He had lost everything, everyone. He'd done it to himself. If only he could go back in time a few minutes!

The best thing was to know nothing. And he'd given up the second best, to know and not tell. It had done him no good. There had been one moment of elation when he'd shouted at his father and delivered himself of the burden of what he'd witnessed on the beach years ago. Now there was desperate regret. What would he do?

A rattling noise broke into the silence and distracted him from his misery. He looked through the back window. A beat-up little foreign car pulled in to park behind him. He could make out an old woman behind the windshield, in the driver's seat. A car door creaked. The old woman stepped out, drawing after herself a large canvas bag. Liam got out of the backseat at the same time, and she saw him and smiled.

Her little teeth, pale yellow like the kernels of early corn, gleamed in a big soft face framed by hair the color of cigar ashes. Thick eyeglasses sat on her fat nose. Her shabby dark coat was buttoned to beneath her chin. She wore hightop black sneakers, and as she came toward him, she favored one broad foot, canting forward with each step.

"You must be Philip's son," she said in a gravelly voice. "I brought his reading matter. It's hard for him to get to the library now and then. How is he? Last week was pretty bad. I'm Mrs. Sigurd Mottley—called Sig for short."

She was standing in front of him, peering at his face. She was shorter than he was. She must be very old. Probably in her eighties, he thought.

"Are you? His son?"

"Yeah," he said. He smelled strong sweet powder. Lilac, he guessed.

"You don't waste words," she remarked. She continued to look at him closely. Could she see he had been crying?

"He's told me about you," she said. "That is to say, he refers to you often in our conversations. Liam, isn't it?"

He nodded.

"I help out here and there. Your father doesn't always get around too easily. We don't have much of a community. Too isolated, only a few people in the winter. I'm in a church group. Very small congregation, but we try to keep an eye on one another."

He had to say something. She was waiting.

"Thanks . . . for keeping an eye on him."

She laughed. "No thanks asked for. Going

around like this keeps my mind off my troubles." She started down the slope to the front of the cabin.

"He showed me a drawing book of his garden designs," her voice trailed back. "Wondrous. What you can do with a hedge here and there." She seemed to be waiting for him. Reluctantly, he walked to her side. He was being drawn back into the cabin. She rested a hand as light as a leaf on his shoulder. "He wants to go to Ireland with you," she said softly. "But you won't count on that, will you? Poor man. AIDS is the pits."

Liam shuddered. His curses came back to him, shouted at a place he'd never been, at a poet he'd never read. But there was a surprise in the way she'd said the name of the sickness so plainly.

She halted for a moment and spread open the canvas bag. "Books about Ireland," she said. "I found him a street map of Dublin. That's all he wants these days. *Gaelic Twilight*—he'll be pleased I got that. Who am I to tell him he won't be able to go? He'd appreciate it if I knew something about Ireland besides shamrocks, and car bombs in the North. It gives him relief to talk about it. He told me his grandfather, your great-grandfather, was a veterinarian in Donegal. I didn't know there was such a place. And the vet packed up and emigrated and came here to settle. Well—it must be dreadfully hard on you and your mother. It would make me cry if I could. But I seem to have lost the knack for crying."

He realized she was the only person besides Aunt Mary and his mother who knew what his father's sickness was. The only person he knew anyhow. He didn't know the doctor who treated his father, or doctors. When old friends of his mother and father's came to the apartment, they didn't say *AIDS* right out as Mrs. Mottley had. "How is he doing?" they might ask.

"You coming?" Mrs. Mottley inquired, her hand on the door.

He would have to go in. Either that or walk to Springton and wait for the bus back to the city. But he couldn't do that. His return ticket was in his backpack.

He followed Mrs. Mottley into the shadowy room, where his father sat in the wicker chair, his head against the backrest, just as he had been when Liam had first arrived.

DURING THE FEW MINUTES Mrs. Mottley talked to his father, she handed him one by one the books she had brought, pronouncing the titles aloud as though it gave her pleasure. Liam leaned against the kitchen sink. Julius wound himself around the old woman's ankles, and, groaning a little, she stooped to pat him. Philip would look at each book and let it fall from his hand to the floor.

"They may turn up that story you wanted by Flann O'Brien, was that his name?" Mrs. Mottley asked. "They've got that system, you know, the computer they can do a search on. But I did dig up a map of Dublin. Here. I thought you'd like it."

"I love it, Sig. You're an angel."

"Don't call me that. It drives my mind toward my failings. Are you all right for everything else now that your son has come? The church is giving a little Thanksgiving dinner tomorrow. I could drop by some turkey."

"Sig, I hate turkey. But Liam?" His father looked over at him. "Will you be here tomorrow? Would you like some turkey?"

Liam said no, not sure which question he was answering.

"Not even apple pie?" Mrs. Mottley asked, looking from Liam to Philip. Then, as though their unanswering silence was of no consequence, she said, "Well, since you're together, apple pie can't count for much, can it? I'll be back next

Wednesday, Philip." She stooped once more to touch Julius's big head before she went to the door with her shambling, forward-leaning walk. She paused there and looked back at Liam.

"I'm glad to have met you," she said in a serious way. "I hope I'll see you again."

After she had closed the door, after Liam heard the car drive away, his father began to speak, tiredly, calmly.

"When she first turned up," he began, "I was appalled. I thought she'd kill me with the sort of goodness you're supposed to praise constantly. But she's not like that at all. She's a smart old person. She's poor as a mouse, lives on a few dollars from Social Security. She used to work in the Springton pharmacy until she retired. She was married once, she told me, years and years ago, but only briefly. No children. No family left at all. I've driven by the shack she lives in. She keeps a few chickens, an old brown dog, and lots of cats. Some of the summer people, the ones who rent houses in July and August, abandon the poor things when they've finished playing with them—like toys—and she gathers the strays and orphans and shelters them. She looks in on sick people, like me—not that there are many around here like me. She's merciful. She hasn't the least idea that she's a hero."

It was as though nothing had happened earlier on the road behind the cabin. How could that be? Liam wondered. How could it be that after such violence of feeling, such terrible words, they were still together?

The room was nearly dark. Liam was thankful for that. A light might dispel the easing of tension between them. He had begun to feel a delicate, mysterious touch of comfort as he listened to Philip.

"And the library books she brings. I'd be lost without them," he went on.

"You said you were going to write about the history of botanical gardens," Liam said. His voice sounded strange to him, faintly rusty.

"Yes, I really was. But I found out it takes physical strength to write. I didn't know that. And you have to have the intention and keep it. I lost that. This sickness interrupts everything."

Julius was purring loudly. "He sounds like Brown's molecules," Liam remarked.

Philip laughed. "It's such a lovely sound," he said. "When I wake during the night, he's there on the cot, weighing two hundred pounds, it feels like, all of it shoved against my leg. I feel desperate sometimes, all that weight on me. But he and I—we travel through the dark together."

He'd been alone until Julius came. Then there had been only a cat, purring, for company. But it was all his own fault.

"Mom and I came—when you'd let us."

"Let you!" his father exclaimed. "What gave you the idea it was up to me?" He seemed to hesitate a moment, to struggle for words. "It could have been different when you did come if you'd talked to me as if I was real."

There was a hardness in his voice, resentment. Liam went to the lamp with the torn shade and turned it on. For a moment he was blinded. "Don't say that to me," he said, and turned to face his father. "It wasn't up to me either."

Philip groaned. "Oh, I know that. What I said was wrong. But, Liam—because something took me by surprise doesn't change everything. I'm your father. You didn't become someone else's son. Your mother didn't vanish from my history. If I could explain what happened, I would. Mom told me you tell your friends I've got cancer. Sometimes she even seems to forget—and tells *me* I've got cancer. But secrets have a way of telling themselves despite the efforts we make to conceal them."

"Why did you come down here? Why did you just leave us?" Liam shouted, startling himself.

"Listen! Every time your mother looked at me, she thought of how I'd wrecked everything for her. Your mother is naturally a kind person—in the same way that your aunt is naturally unkind. Although unkindness seems to have no end, there is a limit to kindness. And I couldn't bear her suffering! I had to get away from it—to keep some strength for myself. And there was something else. . . ." He looked away from Liam and fell silent.

"Did you tell her?"

"As soon as I knew."

"Knew what?"

"That I was sick," his father said with a touch of crankiness.

"I mean—about him."

"I thought, at first, it was a kind of aberration—"

"I don't know what that means."

"A singular thing, a onetime thing."

"But you had to tell her, didn't you? How you got it?"

"We always told each other everything. But this time—I couldn't speak of it until the sickness forced me to."

"So you did tell her, about him?"

His father nodded.

"Why didn't you lie!" cried Liam.

"How? Tell her I was a drug addict? Do you think she could have believed that? And it would have killed everything between us if I had lied."

Julius was pacing back and forth in front of the refrigerator.

"There's an open can of cat food in there. Feed him, will you?" his father asked.

Liam took the can from a shelf and dumped the cat food into a plastic dish on the floor next to a bowl of water. Julius began to eat, purring between bites.

"Liam? Does your mother know what you know? Did you tell her that you saw me on the beach with Geoff?"

Liam, watching the cat, shook his head. "Doesn't she tell you everything?" he asked. "That's what you just said. How come you think she wouldn't have told you that?"

"You never said a word?" his father asked wonderingly. "How have you kept it to yourself all this time?"

"Get off my back, will you?" Liam said. "What do you care?"

"Tell her," Philip said. "As hard as that will be for you both, it can't be as terrible as her finding out you've known all along. Please. Liam, look at me!"

Reluctantly, Liam looked at him. Philip was pulling up one pants leg. There was an irregular blotch like a flattened pinkish leech on the pale skin near his shin.

"That's Kaposi's sarcoma," Philip said. "And it is a kind of cancer. They treat it with a drug that only weakens the immune system further. It's the nature of this awful thing. It's like a nightmare octopus that grows two tentacles to replace the one you cut off.

"What you've been telling people is a part of the truth. I won't ask you to change that story. But you must tell her!"

"I'll tell her what I want to," Liam cried. "And if you say one word to her—about the beach and all and me being there, I won't come here again. Never!"

"Can you tell me why?" his father pleaded.

Liam couldn't answer him. He didn't know why. He only knew that to tell his mother about the blond man was the worst thing he could think

[61]

of except for an imagined scene that came to his mind from time to time—a scene in which he stood up in the school auditorium and announced to everyone that his father had become one of the statistics about AIDS written on the blackboard in the sex-education class.

"How come he isn't here?" Liam asked, his voice shaking with anger. How he hated it all! Grown-ups and their messes!

"He was," his father answered in a low voice, almost a whisper. "I took care of him until he went to the hospital to die."

"That's why we didn't come to see you the first months you were here?"

His father nodded, not looking at him.

"And he's dead?"

"Yes. After a long time."

Liam was silent a moment. A shameful gladness filled him. Good!

"That's who you meant when you said a friend had died," he stated.

"Yes."

"He died from what you've got," Liam said.

"Don't be glad about anyone's death," his father said sharply as though he'd read Liam's thoughts.

"I'm not," Liam said. But he had been. He

[62]

glanced around the room, thinking, *He* was here, sick, getting thinner like Daddy until finally he was too thin for living. A thought struck him. "Would you have left us? Gone away with him if he hadn't died?" he asked.

"I don't know what I would have done," his father replied slowly.

"Don't you know anything?"

"Each time I think that I do, find some knowledge I can grip and hold on to, it's a path opening into all that I don't know," Philip said.

"Even that old woman, Motter . . . whatever . . . knows we aren't going to Ireland or anyplace else. You can't even feed the cat tonight! Don't talk to me about trips anymore."

"All right. I won't," his father said.

Maybe Aunt Mary was right, Liam thought. The world was a leaking sore, and you'd damn well better have your own towel!

When Luther or Delia asked how his father was, he'd answer, "He's doing okay." Sometimes he felt swollen with the lie.

He was thinking now of how it was with Delia when they could find a place, a time, to be alone. He thought of the breath-stopping weight of breast and bone against him. And at such a moment, he'd recall the long arm with its blond down, reaching out of the shadows of the dune to clasp his father's neck. He'd see the broken sticks of the eagle kite that he'd stamped into the sand. Then he'd let go of Delia, and he'd talk to her indifferently, as if she didn't matter to him.

He'd move far away from her into that world of cold talk about sex that went on in the boys' bathroom at school. Or when they were all together, he and his friends, after classes, a small mob moving down the street, showing one another how much they knew, sneering at Harriet Varney, pregnant, famous in the sophomore class because of her huge belly, her grim-faced mother coming to get her every afternoon, laughing cruelly when nasty Eric Bleidel said, "The barn door was locked after the whore got away."

How superior they all felt! Kings of nothing! What if Liam had said on one of those afternoons when they bawled and shouted their way from school, scattering the grown-ups who passed by like scuffed pebbles, "My father is a faggot!"?

He thought he would fall to the floor with the horror of the thought.

"Can't you say anything?" he asked, his voice trailing off.

For the second time that day, his father wept. As tears coursed down his gaunt face, he said,

"You lose your skin between yourself and the world when you're sick the way I am. There's nothing between you and it. I can say—are you ready for supper?"

Oh, God! thought Liam, staring at his father's face. He looks like an eagle . . . a sick eagle.

HIS FATHER WAS FIDDLING with a string bean, turning it over and over with his fork. Liam, who had thought he had no appetite, had eaten everything, cold roast chicken, the bean salad, a thick chocolate brownie.

In Springton, Liam had wandered about the main street while Philip got their supper from the take-out bakery. There were a few stores, the pharmacy where Sig must have worked, a hardware center, a dress shop in whose single display window a dusty wedding gown hung from the shoulders of a mannequin, some ramshackle houses, a small movie theater with one poster advertising an old Disney movie, a seafood restaurant closed for the winter, and a dark narrow pizza place, in its gloomy depths a red neon sign flashing MEATBALLS!

Despite the mournful, half-deserted look of the street, the air was crisp and faintly salty. Liam thought of how it would look in summer, everything open and busy, people strolling with children. He felt he'd been let out of a locked, airless cellar for a little while.

He looked across at his father's nearly full plate.

"Aren't you going to eat any more?"

"I'll try," Philip said. He gave a slight cough. A moment later, he was coughing convulsively. He staggered away from the table and stood in a corner of the cabin. Liam wanted to cover his ears.

The realization of his father's physical suffering entered his consciousness. Until that moment, everything about him, the leech-shaped mark on his leg, the slowness of his movements, had been simply more proof of his father's responsibility for the misery he had caused Liam and his mother.

"Can I do something? You want a glass of water?" he called out.

He thought he saw him shake his head. After another moment, the coughing ceased and Philip returned to the table. He ate one string bean, his face full of distaste.

"The body closes up like one of those sow bugs you find under a board," he said. "Its tiny legs fold in, and it turns into a dark gray ball. No room for food. I'm okay now. I want to say that I know we can't go to Ireland. It's been a wonderful story, a daydream I've been having."

He took a crumpled pack of cigarettes from a shirt pocket and got up and opened the small window over the sink. He stood there blowing smoke out into the night. "Maybe you can come down here for a few days during your spring break," he said.

"That's months away," Liam said. He regretted his words at once. They mustn't talk about "months away." But his father seemed not to have heard him.

"I may be stronger. We might drive south, perhaps to Cape May. Even to North Carolina. Julius likes the car. He sits in the back window and dozes. There are splendid beaches in the South."

They wouldn't be able to go anywhere. Liam didn't want to say that, although the words seemed to press against his lips. He changed the subject.

"Grandpa called last week and I answered the phone. He was okay at first, then he said, 'Who is this calling me?' "

"I'm glad his memory is shot," his father said, his voice a little stronger now. "He would have been so bewildered and frightened by what's hap-

[67]

pened to me. You know he was a mechanical engineer? Not only in his work. He insisted that all trouble was structural. When your grandma died twenty years ago, he shrank into himself. But he worked in a frenzy. I suppose he found comfort in the way things could fit one another and answer a purpose you could see right in front of you. But what you can do with engines you can't really do with living. My mother was sick for a long time. He couldn't solve that, though he felt he ought to be able to solve it. It's when he began to be forgetful."

He had never spoken to Liam about his own father before. Liam strained to understand what he was being told about an old man he had liked but who always seemed to be thinking about something else, not the person standing in front of him. Now his grandpa couldn't think about anything much.

Philip turned on the faucet to extinguish the cigarette. "God! It tastes awful! I think I'll give it up."

Things had changed again. Liam felt the difference in his legs and arms, all through his body; it was an ebbing away of raw strain.

"Will you clean up, please?" his father asked

in the familiar, confident voice Liam had heard all his life, up until a year ago. "I'll take a lie-down for a while. I see the sky has cleared. We can go for a night walk."

Liam carried plates to the sink. His father moved out of the way, saying, "I'm glad you'll be here tonight. And there should be some compensation for you. You won't have to find Aunt Mary waiting behind the door to give you the third degree."

He picked up the small plastic salt and pepper shakers from the table and held them to his eyes as if they were binoculars. "Wickedness is everywhere!" he said in a falsetto voice. "That brother of mine . . ." He faltered, returned the shakers to the table. Somewhat reluctantly, he said, "I'm not being fair."

They looked at each other, both, perhaps, thinking about being fair, what it meant.

"When I was a little kid, I loved Mary so, my big good-looking sister who knew everything. She hasn't spoken to me since I became sick."

Liam hadn't known that. He'd not given a thought to what went on between his father and his aunt, not even thought of them as brother and sister. They'd simply been there.

"She began to be disappointed so early." His father frowned. "Now she's stuck with the care of our old man. I can't lift a finger to help her."

"Does she know about it? How you got sick?"

"Your mom wouldn't have told her. But Mary has antennae. She has suspicions. It's a matter of principle with her, to believe only her own explanations for whatever happens, in her family, in the world. I don't know what she knows— or guesses. I'm so sorry about her. About the two of us, more than ever now.

"We got lost in the woods once. Dad and Mother had taken us to a state park somewhere for a picnic. We wandered off. She's only five years older than I am. But she carried me on her back when I was too tired to walk. I guess she was about eight then. I can still feel it, her braid, my cheek resting against it, my legs hanging down her back. She must have been scared, but she was trying to keep me from being scared. Now I'm lost in the woods again—and she's so angry."

Liam turned on the faucet, holding a plate under the weak flow of tepid water. The sadness in his father's voice was hard to bear. He made himself think of something funny, that time when his father had removed Liam's little cap with the propeller on top of it that whirled when he moved, and put it on the head of Julius's predecessor, a large, solemn orange cat named Sweeney, who died some years past.

Liam smiled, visualizing a cat's indignation when it's made to wear human garments. He must have been about three. Mom was out somewhere. It had been he and his father, laughing together helplessly. He turned off the faucet. The cabin was so silent. Did Brown's molecules sleep at times like everything else? His father was gripping the back of a chair. His hair was as thin as old Sig's.

"I could make you toast," Liam said urgently, glancing at the barely touched food on his father's plate.

Philip raised his head. "I haven't got a toaster," he said, gently as though he were speaking to an infant. He smiled; his eyes seemed enormous to Liam, the way your own eyes feel when you look up at the sky.

"But thank you," he said in a grave, formal voice. He made his way slowly toward his cot.

WHO ARE YOU SUPPOSED to pity? The thousands drowned in a tidal wave in a far-off country you have trouble finding in an atlas? Children starving in places that have become deserts because rain has ceased to fall?

As Liam cleaned up the supper dishes, he thought about himself and Luther and pity. A week or so before, he and Luther had gone to a big record store on lower Broadway to see if they could get a videotape they both liked of a small new band called Slave Ship. Near the store entrance, a man was sitting on the sidewalk with a cigar box opened on his lap. His face and bare ankles were grimy with dirt.

For a second, Liam thought he was the beggar from the church. But it was someone else, much older. He paused. Luther grabbed his arm. "Come on," he said impatiently.

Liam had taken change from his pocket, and he dropped it in the box, which held a few coins, some of them pennies.

"What did you do that for?" Luther demanded as they entered the store.

Liam shrugged.

Luther didn't notice. "He ought to get a job. Some of them make two hundred bucks a day," he said.

"Maybe he can't get a job. He's old."

"Yeah. Well, tough! There are plenty of jobs."

"How do you know?" Liam asked.

"Because I know! I'm not feeling sorry for someone like that. What about people getting killed in earthquakes, that kind of stuff? It's not their fault. That guy screwed up his own life."

In the record-store window stood a full-scale cardboard figure of Elvis Presley in a white satin suit trimmed with gold braid. HE'S BACK! said a sign at the foot of the figure.

"There's someone you've got to feel sorry for. Elvis had everything, and he lost it all."

"Because of an earthquake?" Liam asked sarcastically.

Luther ignored his words. "Look at this mob," he said resentfully. "We'll have to spend the whole day in line."

"God! I hate Elvis Presley!" Liam exclaimed.

Luther laughed. "Don't say that so loud, man. Around here, they'll tear your head off! Elvis is what they know!"

"YOU'VE ALREADY GOT on two sweaters and a jacket," Liam observed.

"The outside of me gets very cold," his father said.

Philip had rested an hour on his cot, his eyes closed, one thin hand upon his forehead. Liam had looked at the street map of Dublin without much interest and opened a few books of poetry. He didn't read in them.

They went outdoors. A streak of black cloud like a line of tar marked the horizon. Directly above, the stars were thick and brilliant.

"When I was lying down, you know what I was thinking about? How you keep things to yourself," his father said. The silence all around them, the chill air like cold cloth, seemed a well into which his father's words fell, distinct, each one like a stone.

"I didn't know what you'd told her, what she knew," Liam said. "But one night I heard Mom say to you something about what you'd done to us. Everything was smoky. I couldn't figure it out. Then I'd stop thinking about it for days—" He fell silent.

"Then—you'd remember what you'd seen on the beach," his father said.

"Yes. I'd sort of remember. When you were in the hospital this summer and you talked about the eagle you thought you'd seen from the window, or the falcon . . . whatever . . . I suddenly thought of that kite you gave me for my birthday."

"What did you do with it? I wondered where

it was when you came back to the cottage that day."

"I broke it. I made a hole and buried the pieces in the sand," Liam answered with a kind of ferocity. It wasn't directed toward his father. He felt clear and righteous as though, at last, he'd been able to claim a truth of his own, an action of his own. There was nothing murky about it.

"How did you put everything together?" his father asked somberly.

"Maybe I wouldn't have. But you went away. Mom was so quiet. When we came here to see you, it was like there was an elephant in the room and you both acted as though it wasn't here. Everybody knows about AIDS now. How you can get it . . . all that. I've just listened to her lie— talk about a blood transfusion."

His father's voice rose sharply. "What's that scorn I hear in the way you're talking?"

"You people. You all lie. In the government, the police, the whole world, lying, lying . . ."

"You lied, too," his father said. "You lied by not saying what you suspected."

Liam was silent. After a moment, he said, "Are we going for a walk?" Trouble was coming back, a little lash of anger, like a wave breaking at his feet.

"The reason you know about everyone else telling lies is because of your own lies," his father persisted. "Do you want me to remind you of the whoppers you've told?"

"It's not the same!" Liam cried out at the injustice.

"Don't get mad. I know it's no way near the same. It's wrong to lie and people do it. It's a kind of choice human beings seem to be able to make even when they're little. Just don't let yourself off the hook."

"Why didn't you tell me yourself? I had to try to figure things out all on my own," Liam heard himself wail. It surprised him as much as it appeared to surprise his father, who froze into a statue.

Was there going to be another fight on the road? It was much too late to get a bus back to the city. Liam saw himself trying to sleep in a cold field.

The statue suddenly moved and held out both his hands. "I didn't know how to tell you," his father said. "How could I explain what I didn't understand?" He began to walk toward the road.

"I've tried to find some part of me that isn't sick," he went on. Liam caught up with him but kept a distance between them. He was stirred and frightened.

They gained the road, and as though they had reached a silent agreement, each went to an opposite side. There was no breeze. Starlight illuminated the dun-colored autumn fields around them upon which fell the shadows of trees like reflections on the surface of a muddy lake.

"Sickness swallows you up," Philip said. "I keep trying to find a thing it can't touch. When I imagined going to Ireland with you, it was a wish to be as I once was."

They walked along the road for a few minutes, not speaking. When his father spoke again, it was in the most dejected voice. "I know we can't really go anywhere."

Liam supposed he had thought being grown-up only meant doing whatever you wanted to do. The things children wanted to do were almost always what they weren't supposed to do. He had thought there was one world for grown-ups, a different one for children. He had thought grown-ups were never helpless.

The misery of the beggar had touched him lightly, not his heart but his curiosity, because he had the same sickness his father had.

Philip was still talking to him from across the road. He listened reluctantly.

"When you were little," his father was saying, "around four, I think, you asked me, 'Do you know about the stars?' I said yes, I knew about them. You were lying on the floor, your chin propped up on a hand, and you asked me then, 'What's behind them?' "

"What did you say?" Liam asked. He had always loved hearing about times when he was very young. Even now, when his head was so heavy, his brain so cloudy and confused, he felt the familiar love of hearing his own history. It was as though he could visit his earlier self and feel what he had felt then.

"I told you that nobody was certain. That scientists, astrophysicists, had ideas about it."

"That would have cleared it all up," Liam said.

His father laughed. "That's my boy," he said softly.

"We've been reading about the universe in school," Liam said.

"And now do you know what's behind the stars?"

"Infinity. The universe is supposed to be growing all the time."

Now his father burst into laughter. "Listen

[78]

to this," he said in the buoyant tones Liam had all but forgotten, it was so long since he'd heard them. "I read in the paper last week that there'd been a supernova explosion that happened fifteen million years ago, but the light from it only reached the earth on Saturday. *Saturday!*" his father shouted into the night. "Poor little earth and its tiny weekdays. Fifteen million years ago!"

He laughed again. Liam, glancing at him, had a fleeting impression that he was strong, that he had been almost restored.

Energy is like a flame, he thought, and even as he said this to himself, his father seemed to be extinguished, to become insubstantial like a shadow.

"Do you believe in God?" Liam asked him suddenly.

"Yes," his father said. Liam was astonished for some reason. He waited for an explanation, for some of the things he'd heard other people say— that God was nature or a universal force or an invisible presence in all life.

His father said, "A Scots philosopher, Hume, I think, said we can't know."

"How can you believe in something you can't know?" Liam asked.

"It's done all the time," his father replied. Liam thought he heard a note of mockery.

"You're laughing at me," he said.

"Oh, no! Not at you. Never at you!"

They stood still, looking at each other. Though they had both spoken with strong feeling, they had kept their voices low. There was something about night in the country that made you feel like whispering.

He observed that his father had his hands in his pockets just as he had. He felt the increasing chill in the air. The branches of a nearby maple looked like a chart of bones, one of those Liam had seen in the medical encyclopedia.

"Have you called me a queer to yourself?" his father asked almost lightly.

"I hate that!" Liam flashed out.

"It's only another word for what isn't understood."

"Can you say how it was? What it was?" Liam asked. He heard a tremor in his voice. Did he really want to know? It was more as if he had to.

"It breaks over you like a huge wave," his father said. "You go under. Some people swim out of the wave. I couldn't. It wounded your mother dreadfully. Sometimes it was worse for her— about Geoff—than the fact of my sickness. She felt I had chosen someone over her. No. That I'd chosen a man over her. But I think it's different now for her. She's had to go through so much.

"I'm not sure of anything, Liam, except that you're here, and I'm glad for that."

Liam could see his father shivering. And his breath, as he spoke, was uneven, as though he'd been running for miles.

"We'd better go back," Liam said.

He turned toward the cabin. When he glanced over his shoulder, he saw Philip following him almost meekly.

They hadn't fought after all. There was some comfort in that. It was as though, finally, they had entered an empty room from which all the old things had been removed so that there was nothing left except bare floor and walls.

Imagining that room, Liam began to put things in it, a poster of a mountain range in Alaska, a big table upon which he could place books and paper and pencils, a chair he could sit on, a good radio, shortwave maybe, a photograph of Delia, her head turned in such a way that her dark hair fell against one cheek.

They were going down the slope to the cabin door when his father spoke. "About the stars. Did you know it's really true—that the light we see is from the past? That when we look up at the sky, all we can see happened millions of years ago? That it took all that unimaginable time for the light we can see now to reach us? It's all in the past. It's all over."

THE CABIN HAD NO SHADES. The moon had risen and pools of light lay upon the dusty floor. Liam had been listening to his father's breathing from across the room. He slipped out from under his blanket on the sofa bed and went to the cot. Julius was lying curled at its foot.

Liam stood motionless, looking down at one of the two most familiar faces of his life, its features sharpened by illness, softened by moonlight.

He thought of the invisible pores of flesh, the caverns of ears and nostrils, the complex, intricate mesh of bone and socket. He thought of entering human bodies.

Language, the capacity to speak, was in a person from the very beginning. Somehow, you knew about what bodies could do, too. Your own body told you. What you did to it and with it told you.

In the classroom with the jolly teacher, even as she wrote out the information, the warning words that appeared so quickly on the blackboard—*blood, bodily fluids, needles*—it met some knowledge that was already in you, that uncurled like a blossoming leaf.

There was the laughter, too, and the rough stuff. Sex was comical even as it was thrilling. And no matter what you knew about it, there was always much you didn't know.

He and Luther, hee-hawing like donkeys . . . Luther saying something like, "Bottle up! Keep those bodily fluids to yourself, boy!"

But all that was funny faded away when Liam glanced at Delia, sitting at her desk. She might turn her head briefly toward him. He would see, and feel like a knife thrust into his belly, the way her eyes were set so deeply in their sockets, see the high cheekbones, the sudden downward sweep of her thick, rather short eyelashes, the puffy upper lip drawn over the lower lip, even the down on her arm. His gut would sink. He could feel it even now as he stood in the cold cabin.

He wanted to touch his father. Even more, he wanted to crawl under the blankets with him as he had years ago when he was little. Tentatively, lightly, so as not to awaken him, he touched his father's shoulder beneath the blanket with a finger, let it rest there a second.

He gazed at a window. The moon appeared

to hold still against the glass. But, of course, it was moving. Everything, the earth, the universe, was moving all the time. The light that glimmered on his father's face had traveled ninety-three million miles.

As he stared down, shadows moved slowly across the blade of his father's nose, across his sallow, sunken cheeks, until, at last, only one ear showed, perfect, pale, like a seashell bleached white by waves over thousands of years.

FOUR

The Plague

Let's skip a Christmas visit. You know it's
not because I don't want to see you. I'm
studying health. It takes all my strength. No
presents wanted or needed. I won't be
lonely—I have so much to do. I asked Mom
to get you something you've wanted, I think.
I'm concentrating on March, when you can
spend a few days with me. I'm making
plans! Love, Daddy

This note to Liam came a week or so before
Christmas. His mother handed the envelope to

him with a preoccupied frown as though she were thinking of something else. He did not quite believe that look of hers. But he did not want to show the note to her. She had already told him Philip wanted to be alone this Christmas. When she said it, Liam sensed she thought it had something to do with her. He knew it didn't.

It was the first written message Liam had received from his father from the outside—from the world beyond home. He was startled as he looked at the firmly written words. He read the note often during the day, in his room, in the kitchen while he was eating an apple, going down in the elevator. He knew what the words meant: *I have so much to do.*

His father was doing something when he sat in the wicker chair, his head against the backrest. He *was* concentrating, trying to get better in his body.

The knowledge of his father's struggle was new to Liam, like the handwriting in the note. It was after he had come home from his visit to Springton that he'd realized Philip was not idle, that it was the life in him that reached out to take hold of the big cat, that reached for books on Ireland. He was in a battle against what was trying to kill him.

He had bought his father a present. One afternoon just before school closed for the holidays, he discovered a bookstore that specialized in foreign books. He had found a collection of Irish folktales. On one side of each page, the text was in Gaelic; on the other, in English translation. As the clerk wrapped the book, Liam imagined how his father would smile when he unwrapped it. He would take it to him in January, when the holidays were over.

Aunt Mary had returned. Seeing her so soon after Thanksgiving made it seem she was living in the apartment. When his mother said, "Philip wants to be by himself," Aunt Mary made no comment.

But she had plenty of comments about other things. Where was the Christmas tree? The good ones would have been bought by now. Why hadn't Liam cleaned his closet in two hundred years? Why didn't he have writing assignments to take to school in January? His teachers must be lazy. Liam spent too much time on the telephone. His friend, Luther, had the manners of a lout—he hadn't stood up when she came into the living room while he was visiting Liam. Why shouldn't they have turkey for Christmas dinner? What was wrong with turkey?

At their mealtimes, she complained about what she called "consumerism." "Buy! Buy! Buy!" she exclaimed. "Nobody knows what Christmas is about anymore."

"It's about charity and hope, too," his mother said on one such occasion. His aunt raged on as though she hadn't heard.

She's like a car whose brakes are shot, Liam thought to himself. He began to watch her with a certain interest.

"How's Grandpa?" he asked once.

"You have no idea what I have to put up with," she replied. "Wait till you grow up and have responsibilities!"

Before he had thought, the words were out of his mouth. "I won't be able to take care of my father when he's old," he said.

She sagged in her chair and said no more.

On a corner a few blocks from the apartment, Christmas trees huddled together as though terrified by the wild howls of music that issued from a boom box on the sidewalk. The men who sold the trees warmed their hands over a fire in a steel drum, darted to customers, then back to the warmth.

Liam and his mother picked out a small pine

tree and carried it home. "What a runt," Aunt Mary said, poking her head out of the kitchen. The old box of decorations Liam had seen every Christmas as far back as he could remember was on the sofa. Liam found a snapshot in it of himself when he was in nursery school. There were little paper angel wings pasted to his shoulders. Who was he then? Were you only one person? Or were you different people who became one person at some point when you were grown-up?

"We'll decorate the tree tonight," Aunt Mary said.

"We'll do it now, Mary," his mother said pleasantly as if she were commenting on the weather. There was no answer from the kitchen.

As Liam separated the strands of tinsel, he remembered how Daddy had stopped him from tossing handfuls of it on the branches of a tree. "When you put each one on a branch, you have to think first about where it should go. It looks very different than if you've just gotten rid of it all, higgledy-piggledy, so you can get at the presents," he'd told him.

He smiled now as he hung a small wood Santa Claus on a branch. His mother was testing the strings of Christmas lights, whose wires were tangled on the floor like sleeping snakes. She must have seen him smile.

"What's so funny? What are you thinking about?" she asked.

"Something Daddy said once."

She replaced one of the dead green bulbs that were supposed to look like pinecones. "I think of things Daddy would say," she said.

Last Christmas, too, Daddy had not been with them. But he hadn't been alone. He had been taking care of the blond man, Geoff. Had there been a tree in the Springton cabin? He felt a powerful impulse to say out loud what he was thinking about.

At that moment his mother plugged in the socket and the twisted lines of lights went on, green and yellow, red and blue.

"It's nearly the best moment of Christmas. When you've tested the lights and they actually work," she said. He felt weak with relief that he had not spoken of his thoughts. He had come close to some danger; he had passed it, but it left a chill, and the living room, with its familiar, somewhat shabby, furnishings, seemed a place he didn't know. Still, it was better in a way than last Christmas, when he'd felt he and his mother might suddenly throw tree and presents out the window.

You could get used to nearly anything, he thought.

"Maybe we should leave the lights on the floor," he said.

"No, we won't do that," his mother said as though he had made a serious suggestion. "But let's skip the stuff that's supposed to be a carpet of grass."

"Okay," he said.

When they'd finished decorating the tree, his mother went into her bedroom and returned shortly, carrying wrapped presents. Most of them, he noted, were for him. He wasn't much interested. It was strange not to really want anything.

"You had a letter from Daddy," she said. "He must have explained why he didn't want us to visit him. He was never crazy about Christmas, and now . . ." She fell silent. There was a blank look on her face. He knew that look—she was feeling something she didn't want him to know. He stifled an impulse to tell her that in hiding what she was feeling, she *was* telling him something.

She began to speak again with a kind of

brightness he didn't like. "We'll go down to Springton in a few days, shall we? When Aunt Mary goes home."

As though summoned, Aunt Mary came to the kitchen door, drying her hands on a towel.

"Poor Father," she said, sighing. "Of course, he doesn't know it's Christmas. But still . . . Well. The tree looks all right. I'm sure it's more than most people have."

"Most people don't celebrate Christmas," Liam said with a touch of sarcasm.

"I was hardly referring to China and Pakistan and such places," Aunt Mary snapped.

HIS FATHER'S PRESENT to Liam was a shortwave radio. Mom had gotten him a few tapes, including a video of the group Slave Ship, which he and Luther had not been able to find that day at the record shop, four sea stories by a writer named Patrick O'Brian, and two flannel shirts.

Aunt Mary picked up the video and turned it around in her hands. "I suppose this is one of those songs that tell you to go out and shoot everybody in sight."

"It's rock, not rap," he said.

Her present to him—she must have found it in a store in ogre-land—was the thickest, woolliest, ugliest sweater he had ever seen. She insisted he try it on for size. "Perfect fit!" she said triumphantly as he pulled it over his head. He felt he'd instantly joined an order of monks devoted to itchiness and slow suffocation.

For a while during the long afternoon, after presents were opened and dinner was eaten, Liam fiddled with the shortwave bands on his new radio. He heard and was absorbed by jazz music from Jerusalem, a British news broadcast, and voices speaking in languages he didn't recognize. As the day darkened, as evening fell, he went to stand idly at the living room window. In other apartments across the street, he saw the flickering lights of Christmas trees, hills of bright crumpled wrapping paper. But the rooms appeared empty of people. He felt dull and tired.

His mother called to him. "I've got Daddy on the phone. He wants to speak to you."

Aunt Mary was looking through a book of quilts Mom had given her and sat only a few feet from the phone. Liam took it as far away as the cord would reach.

"Hello, Daddy."

"Liam, dear," said the faint voice. "Has it been all right? The day?"

Liam wanted to say, Not without you. "It's been okay."

"Did you reach paradise on your new radio?"

"Just England and Israel . . . a few other places."

"We'll have to settle for those places, then. . . . I can't talk for long, although I'd like to."

"Is it bad?" Liam whispered urgently.

"A little setback," said his father, so weakly, Liam pressed the phone against his ear. "Good-bye, my duck." There was a click. Liam waited for the dial tone and hung up. He went to his room as Aunt Mary said, "He didn't want to talk to me. . . . Afraid I'd tell him about our father."

Liam turned to her from his doorway. "You could have asked to talk to him," he said.

"Did he ask for me in the normal, civil way a brother should?"

Liam slowly closed his door, hoping she would not hear the click of the latch.

But he could still hear her, reciting the list of her trials. "My father, for whom I am entirely responsible . . . late papers handed in by totally insufficient students . . . the house that the nurse is far too superior to even dust . . ."

She was leaving on the twenty-seventh. It was something to look forward to. She had never been so cross and disagreeable, even when Liam had come home the day after Thanksgiving and she had followed him from room to room, carrying most of a pecan pie, which, she insisted, he should eat out of courtesy to her, who had made it especially for him.

The day after Christmas, as the three of them ate breakfast, his mother told Aunt Mary she was taking Liam to a winter jacket sale at Macy's. It was news to him.

"I'll enjoy a few hours alone," Aunt Mary remarked. "But I'll put it to use and clean out your fridge. There isn't room for a grape. Liam's old jacket looks fine to me."

"I suppose it does," his mother said vaguely, taking dishes to the sink.

They left a few minutes later. As soon as they were on the sidewalk, walking toward the subway, Mom said, "We've been sprung. She's going tomorrow, thank heavens!"

"Why won't she speak to Daddy?"

She said nothing. He took hold of her arm. "Mom?"

She handed him a subway token. "I don't know why really. I've asked her to write to him. I don't think she has. Not that she'd tell me."

They had reached the subway entrance. "I

hate her for it," she said fiercely. A second later, she cried, "I'm sorry, I shouldn't have said that!"

"Move on, folks," said a man behind them.

Katherine Cormac grabbed the railing by the stairs that led downward. The man hustled by, muttering something. As they descended into an unpleasant warmth smelling of cement and metal, his mother said, "She's not dumb. She knows how impossible she makes herself. And it's real and constant, you know, her responsibility for Grandpa. We've all been shattered by what's happened. It's terrible for you. I'm ashamed I can't seem to talk about it more—" Her voice seemed to plead.

They went through the turnstile as their train pulled into the station. Liam said nothing, and once they were standing in the crowded car, there was no use in trying to talk. What could he have said anyhow? He glanced at his mother; she was holding on to a strap, her face turned upward, her lips moving as though she were continuing the conversation silently.

The relief he had felt getting out of the apartment, and the anticipation of spending some time with his mother, faded as soon as they went into the store. It was a madhouse of shoppers, shoving and elbowing one another around the counters.

There actually was a jacket sale, but neither Liam nor his mother lifted a single one from the racks. They looked at each other. His mother shrugged, smiled. "Well, it was an excuse to get away," she said. "Your old jacket looks fine."

He was standing beside her. Past the people who milled close by, he glimpsed a long mirror in which the two of them were reflected. He was at least two inches taller than his mother. A strange thought came to him—that the tall, very young man in the mirror was actually his own father, that he, Liam, hadn't been born yet, that everything that was to happen was contained in this moment like a seed in a pod. He felt dizzy. His mother gripped his arm firmly. "I think you need lunch," she said.

They ate tacos, standing up at a round counter. Afterward, they walked along Sixth Avenue until the raw wind drove them into a subway station. He was glad Christmas was over.

Aunt Mary announced as they came in that she had made a chicken salad for supper. She hoped that would do. Later, Liam went into the kitchen to get a glass of orange juice. Aunt Mary was setting the table. He watched her. In her busyness, she seemed unaware of his scrutiny.

Her mouth, so often tight with resentment,

was relaxed. His father had said she was good-looking. Her dark hair was lustrous and thick and bound around her head. A few tendrils escaped from the black hairpins he had first noticed when he was small and had asked his father if she'd been born wearing them. He remembered his father laughing as he said, "I hope not!" Her eyes were like her brother's. And she had his eagle nose. He had not realized until that moment how much she resembled Philip.

She looked up at him suddenly. She must have realized he had been observing her. She smiled so faintly, Liam wasn't sure it was a smile.

"Looking over the ruins?" she asked amiably.

"You're not a ruin," he replied. Hope touched him lightly like a leaf. She looked so much like Daddy. Perhaps they were alike in other ways, too, ways he didn't know about. He felt a longing for friendliness from her. From the strain in his shoulders, he realized he was leaning toward her.

"What would you know about ruins," she said brusquely, and turned to the sink to fill glasses with water.

There was little conversation at supper. Aunt Mary asked without interest if they had found a jacket for Liam, and when Mom said no, she remarked that you never could find much at sales.

After supper, the three of them watched an old movie adapted from *A Christmas Carol*, by Charles Dickens.

"Tiny Tim is really too much," Aunt Mary muttered. Liam had seen the movie so many times, his attention drifted away. The actors were buried in their costumes. Only their heads and their faces, which seemed to have been fashioned out of gray clay, suggested there might be living flesh inside the dark frock coats and huge scarves.

Suddenly, as though imposed on the screen, Liam saw naked bodies entwined like the muscular, snaky limbs of a wisteria. He put his hand over his face. He hardly breathed until he heard the click of the television remote. His mother pulled at his hand. He looked at her blankly.

"Are you all right?" she asked.

He nodded. It seemed to him that at that moment they were inside the same thought, that she had seen into the picture in his head, that it was in hers, too.

"Oh—I forgot," Aunt Mary was saying. "There was a phone call." She was removing cushions from the sofa bed in an alcove in the living room where she slept when she visited.

"What phone call?" his mother asked.

Aunt Mary yawned. "It was when you were

out. Some person named Sig. She said my brother had to go to the hospital again."

"Mary! My God! Philip doesn't go to the hospital just to get a pill! How could you not tell us! Liam, go get the address book on my night table."

"He's always going to the hospital," Aunt Mary said resentfully.

Liam stood next to his mother when she called the Springton hospital. His hands were damp. He heard the squeaking of the sofa bed as it was extended on its metal legs. Mom was bent over the phone, and he couldn't see her face. Her arm was trembling.

She spoke, she listened. Aunt Mary smoothed down her sheets. Mom made two more calls, one to the bus company, the second to the Summer Dreams motel, where she made a reservation for three rooms. She hung up and turned to Liam. Her eyes were wide, staring. "There are no more buses tonight," she said. "We'll go down in the morning. Pack a few things. He's very sick. It's bad."

"What about me?" asked Aunt Mary.

"I made a reservation for you. But do as you like. Liam, we'll have to get up at five."

Liam knew it was coming. He felt it as a gathering darkness around their small family. He imagined Julius alone in the dark cabin. But Sig would have taken the cat.

His mother asked him, "Do you know who Sig is?"

"An old woman down there," he answered. "She helps him."

His mother put her hands over her face as Aunt Mary went, very quietly, to the bathroom and closed the door.

AUNT MARY WENT WITH THEM. There was no conversation in the taxi to the Port Authority or on the two-hour bus trip.

They were each locked into themselves, Liam thought. He felt he was a twig being carried on a fast-moving stream. Perhaps that was why the trip seemed the shortest he had taken to Springton.

They walked from the bus station to the small motel. Only two cars were in the parking lot. A red neon sign, raised over the entrance to the motel office, flashed the name, SUMMER DREAMS. The sign was like a swollen vein pulsating in the oyster gray light of this early hour.

Liam's room was next to his mother's. He

didn't see where his aunt went. The room had a smell that was both clean and stale. Until he turned on a light, it had the aspect of a warehouse, perhaps because the furniture was so big. A television set sat on the bureau, and he turned it on. At the sound of a loud hectic voice, talking about some food product, he turned it off. The huge bed was covered with a spread the color and texture of dried oatmeal. In the bathroom, the toilet seat had a plastic cover powdered with dust. A small bar of soap was stuck to the floor of the shower. Liam put all his clothes in one drawer and one of the novels his mother had given him for Christmas on the bedside table.

Christmas felt far in the past. He was barely thinking of what might lie ahead. He noticed things and didn't reflect upon them.

There was a knock on the door. He opened it and his mother stood there, her skin ashen, her mouth tight.

"I won't forgive her for this," she said, looking over his shoulder as though she spoke to a person lurking in the dim interior of the room. "To not tell us that someone had phoned! I hadn't guessed at how angry she is."

Liam hadn't guessed at how angry his mother

was. He was suddenly frightened. Her eyes focused on him. "We'll go to the hospital now," she said.

As she spoke, Aunt Mary, who must have approached them on tiptoe, said in a low voice, "I'll come, too."

They walked silently to the hospital six blocks away, on a narrow road parallel to the main street Liam could glimpse through the backyards of houses. It had been only a few weeks ago that he had looked into stores on that street while his father picked up their supper at the take-out bakery. The line between *then* and *now* had vanished. Time made no sense to Liam.

Two cars were parked in the space reserved for doctors. In the hospital, a receptionist sat at the information desk in front of a switchboard. A large fake plant stood next to a stand upon which rested a few paper plates holding muffins wrapped in plastic. Looking at them, Liam wondered if the muffins were plastic, too.

Breakfast had been hurried. The three of them had stood in the kitchen, eating what they could find. But Liam had no appetite. He felt hollowed out. He heard his mother asking for a Dr. Parikh at the reception desk. Aunt Mary had gone to the large window near the entrance doors. There wasn't much for her to look at except a squat wood house with a lopsided FOR SALE sign nailed to the front door.

"Go sit, Liam," his mother ordered him in a sharp voice. "We'll talk to the doctor before we go up." She waved toward several chairs grouped around a table. A few torn medical journals lay upon it.

A large woman carrying an infant came into the lobby and walked purposefully to a door, which she pushed open with a grunt. The infant let out a thin cry. Then the quiet returned until a short man in a white coat stepped out of an elevator.

"Mrs. Cormac?" he asked, looking from Aunt Mary to Liam's mother.

His mother stood up. "I'm Mrs. Cormac," she said. She put her hand over her mouth as though she feared she'd spoken too loudly.

"I'm Dr. Parikh," he said. He had delicate features, and his eyes were deep-set and dark. A stern haircut had shaped his hair into a black cap. His fingers were long and thin and browner than his face.

He glanced briefly at Liam. When he spoke, his voice was faintly accented. Words seemed to curl out of his mouth.

"Your husband is very sick," he said. "We've been treating the lymphoma with chemotherapy. But it has advanced. It's in his liver, his lungs. You must be prepared. He's not always conscious. We are doing what we can to make him comfortable."

Aunt Mary had turned away from the window. She stared at the doctor. Her hands were tightly gripped beneath her chest as though she were secretly trying to tear something, cloth or heavy paper.

"I didn't know he had lymphoma," Katherine Cormac said. She seemed to shrink away from the doctor. Liam thought he'd gone deaf. He didn't know what lymphoma was, yet the word filled his ears like a soft poisonous wax. He followed the doctor and his aunt and mother into the elevator, which rose slowly, with much creaking, to the second floor, where they got off. The doctor preceded them down a silent corridor.

Liam knew his hearing had come back when he heard Aunt Mary whisper to his mother, "Where do they get these Indian doctors?"

"From India," his mother said flatly.

Dr. Parikh paused before a door. He looked directly at Liam. "Talk to him," he said. "Talk as if he can hear every word you say. I'll be back later." He pushed open the door. Katherine Cormac went in, and Liam followed her.

"I'll wait out here a few minutes," Aunt Mary muttered.

A nurse stood in front of a window. The light was behind her so that Liam couldn't see her face. She came toward them, and he had to turn to the narrow hospital bed.

Philip Cormac looked like an inert, withered child. A tube led from his left arm up and over a metal bar on a stand to connect with a large plastic bag containing liquid. Another tube came from beneath a white coverlet and emptied into another bag half full of a cloudy yellow water. He heard his mother groan. Or was it he himself who groaned?

They stood next to the bed and looked down at his father. His eyes were closed. His mouth was slightly open, the lips like two lines of dusty chalk. They could hear his slow uneven breathing. His skin was blotched and flaking.

"Philip . . . Philip . . . ," his mother called softly.

"Daddy," whispered Liam. His father's eyelids twitched. The chalky lips moved slightly. One eye opened, then the other, very slowly like tiny crinkled shades pulled up by an unsteady hand.

"Hello," he said so faintly it was like thin paper, or a dry leaf, rustling.

Liam and his mother stooped over him at once, both of them listening intently as though more words would follow, as though everything would be made clear now, that, at last, they would understand what had happened to him.

Philip's lids closed again. For a while, they stood there, watching him.

WHEN AUNT MARY ENTERED the room half an hour or so later, she stayed close to the door. She was silent as she stared at her brother. After a few minutes, she left. The nurse was in and out of the room, her hands busy with small quick movements as she checked the valves on the tubes, touched Philip's wrist and his forehead. Once, she took hold of one foot and held it in her hand.

She had a stern, sad face. When she looked at Liam, she did not smile. Unexpectedly, she reached out and took his hand as she had taken hold of his father's foot and held it in a firm clasp for a second.

Philip, like a rudderless boat, drifted in and out of consciousness. Once he murmured, "So dry." Liam's mother held a glass with a bent straw to his mouth. He turned his head away, frowning. She went out of the room then and was gone for half an hour. When she returned, she was holding a bag of green grapes.

She held one against his lips. "Can't," he muttered. She put the grape into her mouth and pulled the skin off with her teeth. With two fingers, she pressed the pulp against Philip's lips. It slid down his chin. She skinned another grape. This time she kept it between her teeth, bent, and pressed her mouth against Philip's. His whole body seemed to strain as he took the grape pulp into his own mouth.

Dr. Parikh came from time to time. Aunt Mary remained outside the room, going from window to window. Liam wandered down the corridor, glimpsing patients through half-open doors. He saw a woman with her plaster-covered leg in traction; a very old man, hunched on the edge of his bed, his head bowed; and other patients lying motionless in their beds. He went down to the lobby and discovered Mrs. Mottley sitting on a chair, her coat buttoned to her chin. She nodded when she saw him. "I thought I'd come by," she said.

"You could come up to see him," Liam said.

"I'll just sit here awhile," she said.

"He's dying," Liam said.

"I know," she said. "The plague has taken him."

He thought of the beggar on the church steps, the boy whose house had been burned down, his father. "There are so many who—" He couldn't finish his sentence.

"Yes. Thousands upon thousands," she said. She touched his arm briefly. "I've got Julius. He doesn't like the other cats, but he's taken a shine to an old Labrador. They sleep together. It's a sight."

He had forgotten Julius.

"I'd better go back," he said.

"Yes," she agreed. "I expect he knows when you're there."

When he was in the room with his father and mother, time stopped. When he went to the bathroom, or looked through the local newspaper in the small waiting room on the second floor, or walked up and down the corridor, passing his aunt without a word exchanged, it dragged interminably.

"I noticed a pizza place when I went to get the grapes," his mother said to him as dusk began to fall. "Go and get yourself some supper there."

"What about you?"

"I'll get a sandwich or something later. I can't leave now."

"Can't I bring you something?" he asked. She shook her head.

In the pizza place he had seen a few weeks ago, where the sign flashed MEATBALLS! he ate half a pizza. The waiter, a boy not much older than he was, said, "Pretty dead around here this time of year." His voice held an inquiry.

The word *dead* stood out like a boulder in a stream. Liam paid for his pizza and ran back to the hospital. The small building was lit up by now. People milled around the lobby, waiting for the evening visiting hours to begin. He took the stairs, two at a time.

There was a different nurse in his father's room, her fingers on Philip's wrist. His mother was sitting in a chair next to the bed.

"Did you get something to eat?" she asked in a low voice.

He nodded. The nurse looked at him blankly before she left. She was young, with a small pouty face beneath her frilled cap.

"I didn't see Aunt Mary," he whispered.

"She's gone back to the motel to rest," his mother said.

He looked at the bed. His father's eyes were half-open. His fingers plucked at the coverlet.

"Daddy?"

"Are you okay?" his father asked in a voice so cracked and small, Liam wasn't sure if that was what he had really said.

"I'm okay," he answered.

Philip's eyes closed. The hand that was free fell slowly from his thigh. The fingers of his other hand, which was held rigid by the needle from the tube, continued to work at the coverlet.

Liam looked at his mother. Their gaze held for a minute. She smiled very faintly as though she saw him from a long distance away. "It'll be soon," she said.

He left the room, went to the bathroom, to the waiting room, back to his father's door, where a small card read *Philip Cormac*. Minutes passed, or hours. A young woman pushed a cart past him, holding emptied supper trays. The pouty nurse sat at the nurses' desk, reading a magazine. The old man he had noticed earlier lay groaning in his bed. In one room, he glimpsed the sludge gray light of a small television set with the sound turned off.

A few minutes after a large clock on a wall

near the bathroom read ten o'clock, Aunt Mary stepped from the elevator. Liam was standing next to the door of Philip's room. She touched his shoulder.

"Is he still alive?" she asked.

Liam didn't answer. He went inside. His mother lay back in the chair, her eyes closed. He looked at his father. His face was swollen. He bent over him, hearing a thin whistle of air.

He went back into the corridor. Aunt Mary was leaning against the wall. Tears ran down her face, like a thin rain falling on a rock.

It had grown quiet in the hospital. How old was his father? he asked himself in sudden panic. When was his birthday? He couldn't remember.

"How old is he?" he asked his aunt.

"Thirty-eight," she said, and covered her face. Liam noticed a small ring on her finger. The stone it held suddenly flashed, and he turned to see a light go on over his father's room. A nurse went in. He followed her.

His mother and the nurse stood close to the bed. His mother looked up at him. She was holding his father's hand in both of hers. As she gazed steadily at Liam, she placed the hand carefully on the coverlet. She walked to Liam and put her arms around him.

"He's gone," she said into his ear. He looked over her shoulder at the bed, at a body that was utterly still. He couldn't bear the weight of his mother's arms. He moved slowly from her embrace. He remembered it was Saturday.

Saturday, a name for a day. It blew away like a wisp of paper in a flame and disappeared.

Suddenly the room was filled with people, two nurses, Dr. Parikh, and Aunt Mary, her tears dried. Liam went out to the corridor. It felt different to walk there. He wanted to be outside the hospital. He felt strong enough to walk miles.

He was filled with relief. The year was gone, lifted from his back like a boulder he had been carrying. He wanted to leave Springton at once, to be back in the city, to see Luther and Delia. School was little more than a week away. He had things to do.

He went to the big window at the end of the corridor. Although the sky was black, the light outside held a faint luminous shine. He saw trees, a few houses, the amber glow of a street lamp, a car moving slowly. He realized with surprise, as though he'd forgotten all about seasons and weather, that it was snowing.

As he pressed his face against the cold glass and heard the tick of snowflakes, he began to cry.

* * *

ORDINARY, FAMILIAR TIME RESUMED like a clock that had been rewound. One thing followed another. Aunt Mary, after making a phone call to her home and then to Pennsylvania Station in New York, said she'd have to leave them as soon as they returned to the city. The nurse she'd left in charge of Grandpa had a family emergency and couldn't stay on after tonight.

Liam and his mother found Mrs. Mottley still sitting in the hospital lobby. When Liam told her his father was dead, she stood up. "Free of suffering" was all she said. She drove them to the cabin in her rattling old car.

On the round table in the chilly dusty-smelling room, Katherine found a note written in pencil on a page of Philip's sketch pad.

She and Liam read it together silently.

Dear Katherine, dear Liam, Cremation for me as we've always agreed. No funeral. Sig will keep the cat and return a few books to the library for me. Please give her whatever she can use for herself or others. My two dears. There's hardly anything left of me. I'm glad to let go of that little bit. Not frightened at all. Tired.

Katherine and Sig made small piles of clothes and dishes and books, a few groceries. Liam swept the floor with a worn broom. After they'd done their work in the cabin, Sig drove them to the motel.

Mom took Sig's hand in her own. "I don't know how to thank you," she said.

"Then don't," Sig said. "I liked your husband, Mrs. Cormac."

They returned to the city. Aunt Mary left them at the bus station to go and catch her train home.

The next evening when Liam answered the phone, an agitated old voice spoke into his ear, "Can you tell me what's happened to my son? Who is this? Mary is keeping something from me." The voice rose to a cry. "Everything is kept from me!"

"Grandpa," Liam said. His mother came to the bedroom door.

"Is it Liam?" the voice quavered. "You'll tell me, won't you?"

He looked helplessly at Mom.

"Liam?"

"Grandpa, he was very sick."

"Lord," said his grandfather. "Oh, oh, he's dead. Awful! That I should live—"

Suddenly Aunt Mary's voice came loudly over the phone. "Katherine, for heaven's sake—"

"It's Liam."

"Why did you tell him?"

He heard sobbing in the background. "Poppa, sit down!" his aunt called out.

"He seemed to know," Liam said.

"He certainly does now!" she said. "Well, the damage is done. All I can hope for is that he won't remember in the morning." She hung up abruptly.

"But he *did* know something," Liam said to his mother.

"You did right," she said firmly. "No matter what kind of a haze he lives in, he would have sensed it. In her own indirect way, she must have told him something—though she'd never admit to that. You told him what he needed to know. Now. It doesn't matter if he forgets it."

But later, Liam cried in his room. Why had he told Grandpa? Whatever his mother said, he'd made trouble. Would life ever get better? Would there come a time when his thoughts would be clear and simple, when this awful tangled mess of feeling would go away?

Two days later, some friends of the Cormacs gathered in the apartment. Aunt Mary had managed to find a student to stay with Grandpa, and she came, too. What Liam recalled later was the moment when one of her black hairpins fell on the cold salmon lying in a platter on the table. He saw his mother carefully lift it off. And in the kitchen, his aunt had looked at him almost triumphantly. "Father forgot," she said.

People spoke to him gently. He must have talked to some of them. He didn't know what he'd said. There was some laughter, some conversation. His mother was pale. She looked calm, but she seemed to have to sit down frequently. Afterward, when the guests left, Aunt Mary washed dishes in the kitchen. As Liam and his mother returned chairs and tables to their accustomed places, they were both transfixed by her loud cry, "Oh, God! It's over!"

The night before school began again, Liam lay sleepless in his bed. He imagined his father's hands. He thought of ash, of dust, and of something less visible, a thing no human eye could see. Dazed with studying death for so long, he got up and stood motionless. It was as dark as a room can be in the city. He set himself the task of gathering what he needed for school. He found socks, underwear, jeans, a flannel shirt, a sweater, unable to see the color of his clothes. He put them on a chair in the order he would dress himself. Books were harder to collect. As though he were sightless, he felt book covers, ran his fingers across pages, and packed what he thought were the right ones in his backpack.

At some point, his fingers drifted across a package on a shelf; he felt the twist of Christmas ribbon around it. It was the collection of Irish folktales he'd meant to give his father in January. He stood motionless, listening. He thought he heard someone wailing in the distance. He touched the wrapped book with one finger just as he had touched his father's shoulder a few weeks ago while Philip Cormac lay sleeping on his cot in the Springton cabin. The wailing ceased. It must have been an ambulance. He did not think he would ever be able to unwrap his father's present, crumple the paper and ribbon, open the cover, look at what he'd written there: *For my father, love from Liam.* He dropped on all fours. On the floor beneath his desk, he found a ball-point pen and wiped the dust from it onto his pants.

He knew what he was doing was strange, but it didn't matter to him. He never reached for the light switch or raised a window shade. It seemed to him that he must do everything in this darkness, that his slow, nearly silent groping for his things would lead him into sleep. The strangest thing of all was his sense that his father watched him, and that if he turned on a light, that presence, which was without weight or shape, would vanish.

When he had done all that he could think of, he crawled beneath his red blanket and fell asleep at once.

FIVE

Revelation

On a Saturday morning in the second week of June, Liam and Luther went downtown to Greenwich Village to look for a pet shop that sold exotic birds. Luther had heard from someone that toucans, parrots, and macaws flew freely about the shop. His mother had warned him that the largest bird she'd allow him to keep in his room was a budgerigar.

"What I'd like is a condor," Luther said to Liam as they emerged from the subway. "Can't you see it? A bird with a ten-foot wingspan following me to school like Mary's little lamb?

It'd be like having your own personal bomber. They eat deer. I could train it to eat people." Luther laughed.

It had been several months since Luther, or anyone else, had spoken to Liam as if he was pitiful. Listening to Delia, a few weeks after his father had died, tell him how terrible he must feel, he was seized with impatience, as though he were being forced to listen to a dull story about someone else. He had wanted to interrupt her, tell her she had it all wrong. But he kept his mouth shut. He sensed that if he said one word, if he told of the unaccountable feelings he had about his father, everything would unravel, and he'd tell her the whole story.

He felt it packed inside of him like a furled parachute, grief and anger and puzzlement. A touch on the rip cord, that one word, would release the whole of it.

At first, he and his mother had spoken constantly of Philip Cormac, always the Philip of past years, when he'd been well. Gradually, their conversations dwindled. Now they rarely mentioned him. And gradually, as Liam woke up and did the things he had to do, he stopped thinking about him. The first mornings of his father's absence, which had filled him with such an ache, were erased like words on a blackboard, leaving only a ghostly mark or two, here and there, beneath the new writing of his daily life.

Last week, he had tried to visualize his father's eyes. When he couldn't, he told himself, He's really dead.

"It's supposed to be closer to Hudson Street," Luther said as they walked along Bleecker Street.

A young man wearing loose soft trousers and only a deerskin vest over his chest was coming toward them. Lined along the edge of the sidewalk behind him, Liam noticed a few small trees with green leaves. Ginkgoes, he recalled. Saved from extinction by Buddhist monks, Daddy had told him. Between each tree, large black plastic garbage bags appeared to lean over the curb like heavy people looking vaguely for their feet. A scent touched the air briefly as the young man passed them. Lilac. Liam thought of Sig Mottley. She wore lilac talcum. Was she alive? And Julius?

At that moment, Luther cried, "Ooh! Liam! Did you see that cute boy?" His voice rose on the last word like the shrill cry of a bird caught in a net. He bent double with laughter.

With no thought, hardly aware of where he was or what he was doing, Liam seized hold of

Luther's thick arm. "Don't laugh at him! Don't *ever* laugh at him!" he shouted.

Luther swung at him and hit his head. They grappled fiercely on the sidewalk. "What are you!" Luther gasped, twisting a handful of Liam's T-shirt until Liam felt his ribs compress. "One of them? A nasty faggot?"

They fell into the street, their limbs tangled, pounding at each other. A car honked. Liam heard shouts from somewhere nearby. He felt himself violently shoved. His face was pressed to the curb, where he tasted something bitter, acrid, damp butt ends of cigarettes. He got dizzily to his feet. A clump of people stood half a block away looking at him with disgust and fear. The driver of the car that had honked at him called out, "You ought to be in jail, you thug!"

Luther was nowhere to be seen. The car moved on with an enraged roar of shifting gears. The people who had been watching him crossed the street and went their way. The young ginkgoes fluttered in a faint breeze. Someone came out of a shop. Others walked along, looking in windows.

Liam had no idea how long he stood there, still dazed, hearing not the echo of Luther's words but of his own. *Don't laugh at him!* What *him*? What had he meant, *ever*?

He went on toward Hudson, pausing when he came to the exotic bird shop he and Luther had been searching for. In the display window, a great scarlet-and-yellow macaw stared at him from one eye. Parrots preened on swinging perches. Birds he'd never seen strutted and squawked and groomed one another. He stared into the depths of the shop, where he could make out a counter, a customer perhaps, a man carrying a sack, probably seeds for the birds. He rubbed his face and felt wetness on his cheeks.

In his inner vision, the eagle kite he had never had a chance to fly spread its paper wings. The living birds in the window seemed a mass of violent color, painful to his eyes.

It was not Delia or Luther, or anyone else, from whom he had most wanted to conceal the source of his father's sickness. It was from himself. The condemnation and scorn he had so feared in others had been in him all along, ever since he had seen Philip embracing the other man on the beach.

He took the subway, rode up in the elevator in his building, found the front-door key in his hand, unaware of anything he had seen along the way, just as he had been unaware that morning one year and seven months ago when he had come home from Riverside Park with his father.

His mother was in the kitchen, reading the newspaper.

"I know how he got it," he said, surprised at the quietness of his voice. The words he had spoken had risen in him like a tidal wave.

Her mouth moved but formed nothing. Her shoulders slumped. He heard her sigh as she folded up the newspaper. Whatever had passed through her mind, she only nodded.

"I saw him on the beach. It was the summer after he got me the eagle kite," he went on. "I took it down to fly it. Daddy was there with the man. They . . . Daddy held him."

"Geoff Chaffee," his mother pronounced slowly.

"Yes. Geoff. He told me."

She looked up at him. "He told you?"

"Yes. He's dead, too."

"I know."

"Did you ever meet him?"

"He worked at one of the sites where Philip had a contract to do the garden planning. I went once. I met him."

Liam pulled out a chair and sat down across

the table from her. "Did you know then about him and Geoff?"

"I don't believe Philip had fallen in love with him yet," she said. "Maybe he had. I don't know." She got up and turned on the flame beneath a kettle. "Even if you try," she said, "you can't tell everything." She paused and came back to her chair. "Because you can't know everything."

"Did Aunt Mary know—about him?"

"She guessed. We didn't speak of it. It was impossible for her to talk of such things."

"What about you?"

"It was a different kind of pain."

"I wish he'd had a funeral," Liam said with sudden intensity. He hadn't even known he'd wanted that. "Was he ashamed?"

"No. I was, at first." She smiled a little grimly. "When you get left, you feel shame as well as anger. But he'd never wanted a funeral. We used to talk a lot at night. It was one of the things he told me."

He was thinking of them, talking at night in the room next to his.

"Why didn't you tell me?" she asked. "I mean, that you knew?"

He thought for a minute. He said, "If I had told you, then it would have been really true."

They were silent for a while. The water in the kettle boiled. She made herself a cup of instant coffee.

"I've been thinking," she said at last. "I don't start my new job until September. Maybe we could go to Ireland for a week. It was where he wanted to take you. There's a special fare I read about last week in the Sunday paper. Just a week. We don't have a lot of money, but Daddy did his best to leave us afloat. I was thinking of sometime in August. Would you like that?"

As she spoke, she reached out and took his hand firmly in hers. Then, as she had when he was little, she pulled gently at each finger.

"Yes," he said.

"There's something I didn't tell you," she said. "About his ashes." She smiled slightly. "I think I did something illegal. I took them to the New York Botanical Garden. It was very early, and I'm pretty sure no one saw me. I dug snow from around the roots of a Japanese maple tree. I sprinkled them there."

"Would you show me the tree someday?"

"Yes," she said.

They went on talking together quietly. It was a day in June, and the light would last a long time.

Paula Fox's most recent book is *Western Wind*, a 1994 Boston Globe/Horn Book Honor Book. She has been awarded the Newbery Medal for *The Slave Dancer*, an American Book Award for *A Place Apart*, and the Hans Christian Andersen Medal and the 1994 Empire State Award for her collected work for children. Others of her novels are *Monkey Island*; *The Village by the Sea*, winner of the Boston Globe/Horn Book Award; *Lily and the Lost Boy*; *Amzat and His Brothers*, illustrated by Emily Arnold McCully; and *One-Eyed Cat*, a Newbery Honor Book.

Ms. Fox lives in Brooklyn, New York.